‘I think it’s a
he said.

Luke reached out a hand to capture one of hers. ‘Apparently I came very close to death in the accident, and when I woke up it was as if I’d never existed before that moment.’ He frowned, as if he was trying to find the right words for his thoughts. ‘In a way, it’s as if I’ve had to invent myself.’

‘Invent yourself?’ Sally was struck by the strange phrase.

‘I had to find out what I liked and disliked, what I was good at. . .’ He shrugged. ‘I had no past to draw on.’

Josie Metcalfe lives in Cornwall now, with her long-suffering husband, four children and two horses, but as an Army brat, frequently on the move, books became the only friends who came with her wherever she went. Now that she writes them herself she is making new friends, and hates saying goodbye at the end of a book—but there are always more characters in her head, clamouring for attention until she can't wait to tell their stories.

Recent titles by the same author:

BOUND BY HONOUR
A VOICE IN THE DARK
SEEING EYE TO EYE
HELL ON WHEELS
SECRETS TO KEEP
NO ALTERNATIVE

FORGOTTEN PAIN

BY

JOSIE METCALFE

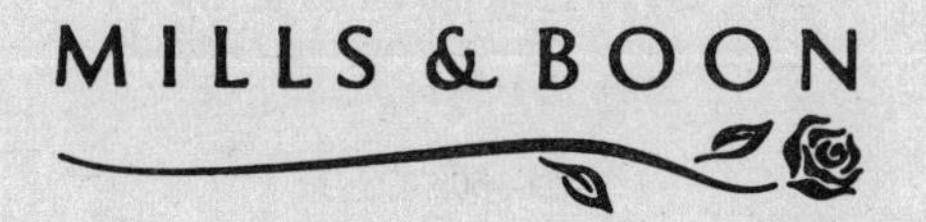

All the characters in this book have no existence outside the imagination of the author, and have no relation whatsoever to anyone bearing the same name or names. They are not even distantly inspired by any individual known or unknown to the author, and all the incidents are pure invention.

Harlequin Mills & Boon Limited,
Eton House, 18-24 Paradise Road, Richmond, Surrey TW9 1SR

ISBN 0 263 79535 7

Set in Times 10 on 12 pt. by
Rowland Phototypesetting Limited
Bury St Edmunds, Suffolk

03-9604-47393

Made and printed in Great Britain

CHAPTER ONE

'DOCTOR?'

In spite of her best intentions, Sally had just been dropping off to sleep in the corner of her big squashy armchair when the phone rang, jerking her back to full wakefulness.

'Dr Webster?' The voice in her ear seemed to reach her from a long way away.

'Yes. I'm sorry.' She blinked rapidly, and shook her head to clear away the cobwebs of sleep. 'Dr Webster here. What is it?'

'Accident at the gravel pits out at Abbey Meads,' the woman said tersely.

'How many involved, and what's the nearest access?'

Sally's feet hit the floor, and she bent forward to search around with her free hand to find the trainers she'd kicked off when she sat down to have a belated lunch.

She forced her feet into them hurriedly as she stood up, stretching the cord of the phone to its full length as she reached for her bag.

'Two mountain bikers racing downhill. Came off a ledge. Probable spinal injuries. You'll have to go out past Priory Park towards open countryside. There's a turning on the left signposted Abbey Meads, and a track almost immediately on the right taking you towards the gravel pits.'

'Emergency services alerted?' The surge of adrenalin meant she was firing on all cylinders now, her brain clear, her pulse-rate elevated and ready to race into action.

'Ambulance coming, with a paramedic on board,' the calm voice confirmed. 'But they have to come across town. You're closest.'

'On my way.' Sally dropped the phone on the cradle and took off across a room cluttered with half-unpacked boxes, barely slowing her stride as she grabbed her jacket off the convenient hook beside the door.

She reached back to grasp the handle to pull it shut, and paused for the rapid scrabble of claws on the polished wooden floor as an eager canine nose followed her out onto the step.

'Come on, then, girl,' she invited, just missing the long plumed tail as the catch clicked shut.

Within seconds she was turning the key in her car's ignition, her free hand reaching for her seat belt.

'Down, Amber,' she ordered, and her companion subsided obediently into the footwell on the passenger's side.

She glanced across at the map spread open over the passenger seat to confirm her direction and set the vehicle in motion, a flick of a newly installed switch on the dashboard activating the flashing green light on the roof.

This was her first call-out since she'd joined the group practice at Abbey Surgery, and she needed to do well. She needed to prove that she'd made the right decision in coming here—if only to herself. . .

The telephone directions were perfect, and she was soon bumping along a rough track leading around the edge of the abandoned quarry, grateful for the car's superb suspension.

'Come on. Come on. Where are they, then?' she

muttered, the chilly wind tugging at loose strands of chestnut hair through the half-open window as she pushed her speed as hard as she dared over the unfamiliar terrain.

'God!' She braked and swerved as a young man leapt out of nowhere, his arms flailing like windmills.

Her tyres slithered to a stop on the loose gravel and she thrust her head out of the window, barely waiting for the electric motor to open it fully.

'What on earth do you think you're—?'

'Down there!' the youth broke in, pointing frantically at a faint track she'd almost missed. 'They're down there. Hurry!' He whirled away from her and disappeared over the lip of the quarry as quickly as he'd appeared.

'Right.' Sally turned the wheel and moved forward gingerly until she could see the state of the track, then increased her speed when she found it was an old access route to the floor of the quarry, wending its potholed way down the side.

By the time she reached the bottom she'd spotted the knot of people grouped round the victims, the buckled remains of their brightly coloured bikes a mute testimony to the event.

'Stay!' she ordered as she flung open her door and took off at a run. The word 'doctor' was emblazoned across her back and she clutched her bag to her chest.

By the time she reached the injured boys both of them were conscious, but one was lying very pale and still, his shattered crash helmet evidence of the severity of the accident.

She knelt down on the gravel-strewn quarry floor, shifting awkwardly as the cold dampness and small sharp stones cut through the sturdy denim covering her knees.

As she cast a rapid eye over the more seriously injured of the two she realised that she would need help with his care. The lower part of his face and neck had taken part of the force of his fall, and she would need another pair of expert hands to stabilise his head while she put a cervical collar on him and maintained his breathing.

At least his pulse and respiration were within reasonable bounds, considering the state he was in.

The distant sound of a siren was drawing rapidly closer as she turned towards the second victim, hoping to have him ready to move by the time assistance arrived for his friend.

'What's your name?' She looked up at the carroty-haired gangly youth hovering over her.

'Adrian.' His voice wavered between tenor and soprano, and his cheeks flamed with embarrassment.

'Right, Adrian.' Later she would have time to smile at his adolescent trauma, but now. . .'I'm going to need your help.' His shoulders straightened importantly. 'Take one of your friends and bring out the two zipped bags behind the driver's seat. Carry them carefully. . .'

He grabbed a husky dark-haired lad by the elbow, and they were sprinting towards her car almost before she'd finished speaking.

As they opened the door of the vehicle there was a low, warning growl from Amber.

'It's all right, girl,' Sally called, barely looking up from her task. She hardly had time to confirm her diagnosis of a broken leg before the two of them returned, and she opened the bags to select the equipment she would need.

A shadow fell over her as the surrounding group of lads pushed forward, and she looked up at them. The concern they felt for their friends was so clear on their faces that it prevented her from snapping at them to stand further back.

'Has any of you done any first aid?' she asked as she glanced round at them with cool blue-grey eyes. Most of them shook their heads, but two raised their hands, as if answering a question in school.

'Right,' she continued, her voice decisive. 'The ambulance is on its way, and we need to get your friends ready to go to hospital. This young man—' She put her hand on his arm.

'That's Jimmy,' Adrian volunteered quickly.

'Thank you.' She nodded. 'Jimmy has broken his leg. He needs to have both his legs splinted together—'

'I can do that,' one of the lads who'd raised his hand broke in eagerly. 'We had that in our test.'

'Good,' Sally praised. 'Take it slowly. Move him as little as possible. Ask me if you need help.'

She turned towards the second still form beside her, steadying herself with a mental reminder to check A, B and C again. She could hear her long-ago instructor drumming it into them. 'Airway, breathing and circulation. . .'

'What's wrong with Wayne?' Adrian demanded.

'He's hurt his face and I think he's hurt his back,' she said quietly as she leant over him and carefully took hold of one hand.

'Wayne?' Her voice was soft but carried clearly in the still air. 'Can you hear me?'

'. . .ss. . .' she heard, and tightened her hand gently.

'Good,' she encouraged. 'Can you squeeze my fingers?' She waited for a response while she noted down the figures for his respiration and pulse, and was rewarded by a deliberate pressure. 'Well done. What about the other one?'

She was just taping the IV line to the back of his hand when her concentration was broken by the hurried arrival of two large pairs of feet topped by dark navy trousers at the edge of her vision.

'Where do you want us, Doc?' one of the men panted as he lowered the stretcher he was carrying to the ground. 'We had to leave the vehicle up on top.'

She looked across at the blond owner of the cheerful voice, his eyes as blue as the shirt of his uniform showing between the edges of his brightly flashed jacket.

It took very few words to direct him towards loading Jimmy and carrying him back up the hill with the willing assistance of his friends.

Before Sally had time to turn her attention to Wayne, the second paramedic knelt down swiftly on the opposite side.

'He needs a neck-brace.' The deep voice was accompanied by a searing gaze from tawny eyes, and for just a moment Sally was unable to look away. The man's breathing seemed unaffected by his rapid descent to the quarry floor, the only sign of his exertion the rumpled state of his dark hair.

When he looked back down at the young man between them on the ground, she was left with a strange feeling of breathlessness before his forceful words finally sank in.

'Of course. . .' She began speaking, then stopped. There was no point in telling him that she fully intended to protect young Wayne's neck because he had already taken a cervical collar out of his kit and was preparing to position it.

'Hold his head without touching his jaw,' he instructed, his deep voice curt as he concentrated on his task. 'He's bleeding from his nose, so we can't do a blind nasotracheal intubation, and he's partially conscious so we can't do an oesophageal. . .'

Sally subdued her momentary surge of resentment at his high-handedness with the silent reminder that it was the patient who mattered, not her pride.

A little imp of mischief had her watching his technique critically, but his procedure was faultless—as was his management of the boy's transferral to the scoop.

'When we've got him strapped down, we'll load him into your vehicle,' he said decisively, barely glancing in her direction as his hands moved competently about their business. 'It'll save time, and your four-wheel-drive will smooth out some of the bumps.'

By now Sally was gritting her teeth, but there was little she could do in front of their avid audience. But, she promised herself, once their patient was safely delivered. . .

The stretcher was locked securely in position in the back of the vehicle she'd had specially adapted, and Sally was stowing her bags behind her seat, when there was a warning growl from Amber.

Glancing over the head-restraint of the front passenger seat, she was treated to the unusual sight of her one-woman dog sniffing at a lean male hand, and she straightened up in time to see his head disappear into the vehicle.

'What do you think you're doing?' she snapped as she wrenched her own door open, resenting this further evidence of his intrusion into her territory—both physical and professional.

'Travelling with you to monitor the patient—unless you intend me to do it while I run along behind.' Sarcasm filled his voice as he swung his long legs round and tucked his feet carefully beside Amber, his reassuring words to the dog spoken in a totally different tone from the one he'd used with her.

'Of course,' Sally muttered under her breath, and bit the inside of her lip as colour surged up her face at her own stupidity. What on earth was it about this man that seemed to rub her up the wrong way?

Admittedly, her recent heartbreak meant that she was less than happy with the male half of the human race at the moment, but she had managed to keep her antipathy under control in a work situation until she'd met *him*—or was there another reason for the sparks flying between them?

The journey up the winding track called for all her attention; the gravel had been loosened by the recent winter of rain and storms, causing her wheels to spit stones in all directions as she guided the vehicle steadily upwards.

From the corner of her eye she was conscious of her passenger turning towards her, and she tensed, expecting him to make the same sort of chauvinistic comment that most men made about women drivers. When he remained silent she glanced across quickly, to find that instead of watching her driving he'd reached one hand back to offer silent reassurance to their patient.

They lurched their way to the top of the quarry to discover that the ambulance had already left for the hospital, and it wasn't long before Sally had reached the metalled road and was pointing the vehicle back towards the town.

Beside her, the silent paramedic was one-handedly noting his findings on the checklist clipped to his board, his pen moving swiftly to fill in the columns of sequential observations. Once they reached the hospital, the duplicate copy would be handed over with the patient to form the start of his case-notes.

'Stop!'

The sharp command broke into her concentration, and she automatically put her foot hard on the brake.

'What. . .? Why?' But her words were spoken to his back as he flung himself out of the vehicle and wrenched the back door open.

By the time Sally reached him he was crouched over Wayne's unconscious body, probing the base of his throat, a fresh pair of gloves covering his long-fingered hands.

'What—?' Sally began.

'Apnea.' His voice was distracted for a moment as he concentrated on what he was doing, giving Sally time to register that Wayne had stopped breathing. 'Either his larynx has swollen or the rough track has shifted something to press on his trachea. . .' He paused to reach into the opening of one of her bags, and withdrew a familiar instrument.

The blade was exposed and the incision performed in less time than it took to blink, and he was inserting the tracheotomy tube in the neat hole he'd made into Wayne's trachea before the significance of what he'd done dawned on her.

'Dammit, you're a paramedic,' she snapped. 'You're not allowed to do a cricothyrotomy.'

There was a frozen second before his eyes snapped up to meet hers, blazing.

'He's alive, isn't he?' He looked back down to tape the tube into position and dispose of the used scalpel blade.

'That's not the point,' Sally argued. 'Paramedics aren't trained to perform surgical manoeuvres. What you did was illegal—'

'But essential,' he broke in, his voice hard. 'Like getting him to hospital.' Pointedly, he looked back down at Wayne, his hands moving surely over him as he checked his vital signs again.

Her back teeth gritted angrily together, Sally backed out of the vehicle and climbed behind the wheel, reaching across to pull the passenger door shut before she put the engine into gear. In her rearview mirror she could see him change position so that he could travel safely beside their patient for the rest of the journey.

Sally activated the siren and flashing lights as soon as they encountered the start of the traffic, the ululating sound only slightly muted when she closed her window up tight as she radioed their position through.

They had nearly reached the hospital when the thought which had been going round and round in her brain surfaced—the life-saving manoeuvre he'd done had been textbook perfect, and he'd performed it as if it was second nature to him.

'Where were you taught to do a cricothyrotomy?' The words emerged unannounced into the intimate space of the vehicle, clearly audible in spite of the noise of the siren.

Her eyes flicked up to the mirror and caught the fleeting reflection of a bitter expression on his face before it was wiped smooth.

'I watch a lot of television.' His deep voice was as mocking as the twist to his mouth, but there was no time for Sally to challenge him as she drew up outside the hospital emergency entrance.

The ambulance which had transported Jimmy had warned the staff of what was coming, so that Sally's radio confirmation of their estimated time of arrival had hardly been necessary.

As she pulled up under the sheltering portico willing hands swung the back door open and unlocked the gurney. Within seconds Wayne was whisked inside, and Sally was left to move her vehicle away from the emergency area.

By the time she rejoined them inside, the paramedic had all but finished detailing his observations, and Sally waited a moment while a set of X-rays was ordered.

'Melanie Scott.' The stocky, greying woman was finally free to turn towards her to introduce herself properly. 'I'm one of the new breed of casualty consultants.'

'Sally Webster.' She shook the proffered hand. 'I'm pleased to meet you—I was told about your appointment when I came for interview.'

'That was a beautiful job you did on the lad.' The older woman gestured across at Wayne, then smiled up at their silent companion. 'Textbook job, wasn't it?' she praised. 'I hope you were in a position to watch her technique?'

There was an awful silence as Sally fought with her conscience, her eyes drawn helplessly towards the deep tawny-gold of his.

She knew she should report the fact that the procedure had been performed illegally, but. . .

As she watched a dark shadow of desperation, almost pleading, filled his eyes, and she found herself unable to say the words which would, in all likelihood, cause the end of his career.

It wouldn't matter that his quick thinking had probably saved Wayne's life. The only thing that would count in the inevitable inquiry would be that he was not authorised to perform a tracheotomy.

Sally gave an involuntary shake of her head and turned towards Melanie Scott, deliberately putting him out of sight as she spoke. 'It had to be done,' she said ambiguously. 'Hopefully that situation won't arise again—it can be very nerve-racking out in the middle of nowhere.'

For several minutes, while they waited for Wayne's plates to be developed, they chatted about Sally's impressions of the area, their eyes busy monitoring as the young lad was expertly readied for transfer up to surgery.

Sally had the strange feeling that she was being watched, and glanced surreptitiously over her shoulder.

For some reason she had expected to see the tall, silent paramedic's blue uniform, and she was annoyed by her disappointment when she found that he had apparently disappeared from sight.

Not long after, she made her farewells and walked towards the plate glass automatic doors. She paused on the paving as they swished smoothly closed behind her to draw in a deep breath of the late afternoon air, dropping her head back and rotating her shoulders as weariness gripped her again.

She'd driven a long way yesterday, with her newly delivered vehicle piled high with the last of her belongings, and it had long been dark by the time she'd arrived.

This morning had been spent unpacking and organising as much as she could before she was due to start on her round of normal practice duties. Little had she expected that she would be called out so soon after her arrival.

Her vehicle was parked in the small overflow staff car park just round the corner of the building, and she had nearly reached it before she realised that she must have left it unlocked in her hurry to follow Wayne into the unit.

The passenger door stood wide open to accommodate a pair of navy-clad legs, dangling sideways over the front passenger seat.

The realisation that she had found her ertswhile passenger stopped her in her tracks for several long seconds as a mixture of emotions assailed her.

She ruthlessly squashed down the rising feeling of pleasure that he hadn't just disappeared when he'd left the casualty department. She was determined that she wasn't going to allow any fleeting attraction towards Mr Tall Dark and Handsome to deflect her from finding out just what he was playing at.

Her well-worn rubber-soled shoes made almost no sound as she started to stalk towards him, unreasonably incensed by the fact that Amber was looking up at him in adoration, with her head resting on one lean thigh. Her expression was nothing short of blissful as he alternately scratched her ears and stroked her silky head.

'What are you doing in there?'

Unfortunately tiredness made her voice scratchy, and her challenge merely sounded petty.

'Waiting for you, of course.' His voice, on the other hand, was the epitome of sweet reason—leaving her once again feeling foolish.

'Why?'

'Why not?' He stood easily, and tucked his hands into the back pockets of his uniform trousers, his jacket pulling open to reveal the width of his pale blue shirt. 'It was the easiest way of making sure I didn't miss you when you came out, and I was able to keep your patient dog company. . .' He shrugged.

'Why did you want to see me?' She folded her arms defensively. She knew it was stupid, but somehow she felt threatened by his size now that they weren't working. She was relatively tall for a woman, at five feet eight, and her slender build belied the stamina and strength she had purposely built up to cope with the demands her voluntary work would impose on her.

He was probably only five or six inches taller than she was, but every inch was tautly muscular. The breadth of his shoulders and depth of his chest were clearly outlined as the same chilly spring breeze which teased at the loose tendrils of her chestnut hair also flattened his shirt against his body.

'I never introduced myself.' He took a single step towards her and offered his hand. 'Luke Nemo.'

For a moment Sally stared at the dark strength of his hand as if she didn't know what to do with it, her glance flicking up towards his watchful tawny gaze as she hesitantly advanced her own paler fingers towards him.

As their hands made contact for the first time a strange sensation made her breath catch in her throat, and as she gazed up at him a fitful gust of wind flipped a dark swath of hair across his forehead.

As he raked his free hand roughly through it he revealed a deep, vicious scar which zigzagged its way along his temple until it disappeared in the thickness of his hair on the side of his head.

Sally gasped, her eyes riveted by the evidence of such an injury.

'What happened?' Her hand tightened around his in empathy.

'An accident.' He shrugged dismissively, pulling his hand away from her grasp as though rejecting her sympathy.

'Obviously. But what happened?'

He shrugged again. 'No idea,' he said flatly.

'But. . .'

He glanced around quickly, almost furtively, before he made an impatient gesture.

'Look.' He glanced down at the plain steel watch strapped around his wrist. 'This isn't something I want to talk about when anyone could come round the corner. . .'

'OK.' Sally gestured towards the waiting vehicle. 'I'm off duty now—barring call-outs. I'll provide transport and coffee.'

She blinked when she heard her own words, surprised at the uncharacteristic impetuosity. It wasn't the way she would have behaved just a month ago. . .

'Why?' The question emerged after a long pause.

'Why not?' she challenged, fixing him with her blue-grey eyes and reminding herself that she wasn't the same Sally Webster any more. Suddenly she was aware of just how much she was hoping he would accept her invitation.

Her heart sank when he gave his head a tiny shake, then soared unaccountably when he turned to step up into the passenger seat.

'I suppose I owe you that much for covering my back in there just now.' He flicked a glance towards the casualty department, then reached out his hand to pull the door closed.

'Well,' Sally muttered indignantly under her breath as she rounded the back of the vehicle, 'don't do me any favours. . .!'

For several minutes they travelled in silence, and she began to wonder what on earth had prompted her to invite him to join her. As she racked her brain for some innocuous comment to break the ice she glanced towards him sitting so silently beside her.

There was such an air of quiet containment about him that at first sight he seemed almost placid. Sally had already learnt better. Underneath he was as full of tension and potential energy as a high-power electric cable. The crazy thing was, she was very tempted to touch, just to see what would happen. . .

She gave herself a mental shake. Crazy was the right word. She hadn't moved all this way to get herself tangled up with anyone—especially since she'd hardly been in the area for twenty-four hours.

It didn't matter that Luke Nemo was easily the most fascinating man she had ever met, she lectured herself sternly. After the fiasco she'd left behind, she'd sworn off men for the foreseeable future.

She was here to work.

Her silent lecture to herself seemed to do the trick, and the remainder of the short journey to her new house was easily filled with answers to his questions about the design of her vehicle.

'The suppliers were fantastic,' she enthused. 'I told them what I needed, and they drew up a plan and then fitted the whole thing out for me.'

'It's been beautifully done.' Luke twisted round to admire the clever use of space in the rear compartment. 'Must have cost a bomb.'

'I'd got some savings put away, and decided this was a really worthwhile project to spend the money on.' She made certain her tone was positive, refusing to allow the familiar heaviness to settle inside her when she remembered why she had been saving up.

'Can you let Amber out your side?' Sally asked as she reversed neatly into position in her drive. 'She'll take herself for a quick visit in the back garden and come to the back door to be let in.' She reached back between the seats to retrieve her bag, then circled the vehicle, checking the doors and windows.

Within a couple of minutes the coffee-pot was steaming and Amber was busily chasing her feed bowl round the kitchen floor as she licked it clean.

'Make yourself comfortable,' Sally invited pulling out a chair from the table as she deposited a jug of milk and two heavy pottery mugs in the centre. 'Sugar?'

Luke turned away from his contemplation of the sadly barren garden in the declining sun and lowered himself onto the chair, stretching his legs out under the table and crossing them at the ankles.

'Black or white?' Sally held the pot poised over the first mug, ready to pour.

'I drink it black first thing in the morning, to get my eyes open, but the rest of the day I like to dilute the caffeine a bit.' He smiled as she nodded wryly in agreement.

'The time that gets difficult is when you get called out and you don't know whether it's going to be the last call of that day or the start of the first one of the next day! The problem usually solves itself, because there's rarely enough time to drink any coffee anyway. . .' She pulled out a second chair and sat down, resting her elbows on the table with her coffee-mug cradled between her hands.

Luke raised his mug and sipped, the steam wreathing its way up past his tousled hair. The last rays of sunshine angled in through the uncurtained window, striking mahogany gleams across his head and drawing Sally's eyes to the start of the scar at his temple.

'How *did* you get that?' she prompted, and saw his fingers tighten instantly around the mug. She held her breath, half expecting the pottery to shatter, sturdy as it was.

After several taut seconds the whiteness over his knuckles faded, and he drew in a deep breath and blew it out slowly.

'Apparently. . .' His voice emerged as a gravelly rasp, and he took another swallow of coffee before he continued, 'Apparently I was involved in a serious car crash, and completely lost my memory. As is often the way with these things, I don't remember anything about what happened. . .'

'You can't even remember the impact?'

He shook his head once. 'Nothing.'

'Did the doctors say whether they think you'll remember eventually? How long ago did it happen?'

'Four years, give or take a few weeks.' He shrugged.

'What about the other drivers? Or bystanders? There must have been witnesses. . .'

'They couldn't even tell the police whether I was in one of the cars or if I was one of the people they ploughed into.'

'Didn't anyone know you or. . .or recognise your name? Surely the police were able to find out? Didn't they put your photo in the papers or on the television?'

'Ha!' He gave a harsh bark of laughter. 'Obviously not even my own family recognised me—the state I was in when they'd finished wiring me back together. Either that, or they didn't want to know.' His mouth shut into a tight angry line, the paleness around his well-defined lips evidence of the tension the conversation was causing.

'But. . .' Sally faltered. 'What about your wallet? You must have had some form of identification on you. . .' Her words trailed away as she saw the slow shake of his head. 'Nothing. . .?'

She was struggling to understand the enormity of what he was saying. 'Your name.' She grasped at the only straw left. 'Surely the police could use your name to trace you?'

He smiled gently, one dark eyebrow raised in a mocking arc until it nearly reached the comma of dark hair tumbled forward onto his forehead.

'Think about my name, Doctor. You know enough Latin for that, don't you?'

She gave an involuntary gasp of horror as the full significance of his name finally dawned on her.

'Nemo,' she whispered. 'Nobody. . .'

CHAPTER TWO

SALLY dropped her head forward and raised both hands to massage the sore muscles in the back of her neck, her elbows braced among the piles of paperwork on the desk.

Out of the corner of her eye she could see her coiled up stethoscope and the calibrated case of the sphygmomanometer waiting to be tidied away.

'I'm as exhausted as I was during my training,' she moaned as she slowly straightened her shoulders and neatened the stack of patient records she'd just finished entering into the computer, conscious of the same sense of bone-deep weariness.

During the past week she'd hardly had time to breathe, let alone sleep, intent only on establishing herself in the practice as well as completing the move into her new house. She would never admit to herself just how much energy she had wasted trying not to think about Luke Nemo.

'Gone eight o'clock,' she groaned as she caught sight of the time and heaved herself out of the chair to turn off the lights. Her stomach rumbled noisily, reminding her that she'd missed lunch—again.

Her morning surgery had spread until it had almost overlapped the early afternoon antenatal clinic, and her list of house-calls had lasted right up to the start of evening surgery.

Not only had she been faced with the usual run of childish ailments and general injuries, but she'd also seen a forty-six-year-old woman who had found a breast lump two years after a lumpectomy, and taken blood samples from a very pale, listless twenty-seven-year-old who had sported some horrendous bruising.

She had her fingers crossed that she was wrong, but from her observations and his own description of the onset of symptoms she was horribly afraid that it was leukaemia.

Sally paused at the receptionists' station to consult the roster, then switched the phone through to the GP on call for the night. She'd hardly met Gareth Evans yet, as his clinics hadn't coincided with hers, but the receptionists spoke well of him—as did the few patients who'd mentioned him.

About her own predecessor, the newly retired George Lavenham, there'd been an uncomfortable silence—almost as if they blamed her in some way. . .

She pulled the door shut and locked it carefully. She knew the drugs were safely secured in the small pharmacy, but there was no sense in inviting trouble from thieves.

The streetlights gleamed on the chrome trim of her vehicle on the other side of the small car park, and as she turned to walk towards it the dark outline of a man straightened up from his position leaning against the side of it.

Her feet felt as if they were rooted in the ground, her hand tightening convulsively around the bunch of keys as fear paralysed the scream she ached to release.

His steps were silent and vaguely menacing in the shadows as he began to walk towards her.

'What's the matter?'

The deep voice reached her before he did, and she nearly collapsed with relief when she recognised it, her keys hitting the ground with a metallic clatter. Only sheer force of habit had her hanging on to her precious bag.

'Don't *do* that, dammit! You nearly scared me to death!' Her voice shook as her heart seemed to pound at the base of her throat. 'I thought. . .I thought. . .'

She shook her head and crouched down to retrieve her keys, her hand still trembling noticeably as she fumbled to pick them up.

'God, I'm sorry.' Luke crouched swiftly in front of her to grasp the keyring. 'I thought you knew who it was.' His hand cupped her elbow as he helped her to her feet.

'How could I?' she snapped peevishly in the aftermath of the surge of adrenalin. 'I haven't got X-ray eyes, and in case you hadn't noticed it's almost dark.'

'Now I'm disappointed.' She could hear the hint of laughter in his voice, in spite of the fact that she couldn't see him clearly. 'I was sure that it would be a case of once seen, never forgotten. My ego is mortally wounded!'

'Ha!' Sally managed as she turned towards her vehicle, her pulse racing for a different reason as she started to walk the last few yards as briskly as if she wasn't aware that his hand was still cupping her elbow.

'Here. . .let me.' He leant forward to unlock the passenger door, and as he pulled it open the courtesy light came on, bathing the two of them in a golden pool and waking Amber from a sound sleep.

Sally went to step up and paused, shaking her head.

'What am I doing?' She turned back to face him, finding herself trapped between the open door and his tall, muscular body. 'I can't drive home from this side of the car. . .' The words faded away to nothing when she saw the smile on his face.

Gone was the grin that went with the jokes; this one was gentle, caring.

'I'll drive you home,' he offered. 'You're tired.' And he ran the tip of one finger across the delicate skin under one eye.

Sally had first noticed the dark shadows several days ago, and she knew that her hair was straggling out of its once smart knot. For a moment the feminine side of her was angry that she was looking less than her best, and that he had drawn attention to the fact. It was several seconds before she recognised the tenderness in his touch, and for the first time in nearly two months she felt as if someone really cared about her.

'How will you get home after you drive me?' she demanded half-heartedly, already turning away to climb aboard and murmur a greeting to Amber.

'I'll walk.' He handed her the seat belt and shut the door, circling the front of the vehicle to let himself in the driver's side.

'You can't. It's nearly two miles to get back here, and it's threatening rain. . .'

She stopped in confusion when his laughter rang out.

'There you are! I knew you cared. . .!' He leant forward to turn the ignition, and the engine started with a thoroughbred growl.

'Luke. . .' She put her hand over his on the gear lever to stop him from moving it. 'It doesn't do anyone much good to get soaked on a long, dark walk—especially this early in the year.'

'Ah, but a quick run followed by a warm shower would probably do me a lot of good.' He threw her a wicked grin as he parodied her words. 'Especially as I only live round the corner from you.'

'You. . .' She doubled her hand into a fist and thumped his arm. 'You were just trying to cadge a lift home,' she accused him, the light-hearted banter lifting her spirits. 'Well, then. In that case—' she settled herself back in the comfort of her seat '—take me home, James,' she said in her haughtiest tone.

'Certainly, madam.' He touched the peak of an imaginary cap. 'At once, madam.' And he set the vehicle in motion.

As he drove Sally watched his cool competence, appreciating his skill with an unfamiliar vehicle.

'You have got a driver's licence, I suppose?' she said idly into the near-dark, and watched him stiffen in the light of a passing streetlamp. She bit her lip, realising how cruel the question had sounded.

'Luke Nemo has,' he replied at last. 'UK, Continental and International.'

'Oh.' Sally subsided, her impulse to apologise squashed by his curt tone.

They were silent for the rest of the journey, and when he'd finished reversing into her driveway she was surprised that he didn't immediately climb out.

Her hand ready on the handle, she turned back towards him when she realised that he wasn't moving. He was staring sightlessly out of the front windscreen, with his hands resting on the curve of the steering wheel.

'Luke?'

In the dimness she saw his head turn.

'I'm sorry. . .'

'I'm sorry. . .'

They spoke together, then halted, each gesturing for the other to continue.

'I'm sorry for snapping at you like that.' Luke finally took the initiative. 'It wasn't necessary. . .'

'No. It wasn't your fault. I'm sorry for asking such a stupid question in the first place.'

'Not at all. It's perfectly reasonable to ask when someone's driving your car,' he pointed out.

'Except when you know he's an ambulanceman,' Sally objected. 'I should have known you would have been properly qualified—I just didn't realise how far you'd taken it.'

They subsided into a slightly uneasy silence, and she mourned the easy banter they should have been sharing.

'Cup of coffee?' she volunteered hesitantly. 'Unleaded, if you want.'

'OK. Thanks.'

Until he accepted, she hadn't been aware that she was holding her breath. She released it in a silent rush.

'Come on, then, Amber.' She turned away, in case he saw the pleasure which was drawing at the corners of her mouth, and opened her door.

In spite of the fact that she had so much still to do to organise her little house, and that she desperately needed an early night, she hadn't been looking forward to the loneliness which would have greeted her as she opened the front door.

Oh, she had Amber, and the dog was a wonderful companion, but. . . But it wasn't enough, dammit!

There would be a cosy familiarity about their sitting together at the kitchen table again, their hands cupping the same steaming mugs while Amber chased her bowl around the floor.

'You need some plants.' His voice broke into the silence, and she looked across at him in surprise.

'Plants?'

'Something green and growing, to bring this room to life.'

'I don't have time to look after plants. They'd all be dead within a couple of weeks.' She grimaced.

'Not if you chose the right ones,' he insisted. 'Some need very little attention to thrive—in fact, they prefer it.'

'Sounds as if you're talking about silk or plastic ones,' Sally joked. 'I'd probably be the first person to have a plastic rose die of greenfly infestation.'

His deep voice rang out in a husky laugh which seemed to curl around her inside, making her feel. . . sort of comfortable. His tawny eyes gleamed with humour, small lines radiating from the corners as though he had once laughed often.

'Would you trust me to find some plants for you?' His words followed easily into the relaxed atmosphere.

'Well. . .' Sally screwed up her nose doubtfully. 'On condition that you promise to rescue them the minute they fall sick. I'm only qualified to resuscitate humans.'

They finished their coffee and she offered him a refill, loath to lose his company so early in the evening.

'How are you getting on at the practice?' he asked as he slouched back in his chair. 'Have you settled in?'

'Yes and no.' She gazed down into her mug as she sorted through the impressions of the last week, then raised her eyes to meet his. 'I love the area, and on the whole everyone has been very welcoming, but—' she gave an exasperated huff '—I feel as if I'm being blamed for something. . .' She shook her head in confusion.

'You took over George Lavenham's patients?'

'Yes,' she confirmed. 'He retired recently, and they needed another willing body to share the load.'

'Has anyone told you why he retired?' One dark eyebrow was raised in query.

'Ill health, I was told.'

Luke gave a wry smile.

'Perfectly accurate, if you're into euphemisms.' At

her startled expression, he continued, 'His wife died about six months ago. Cancer. He managed to hold it all together until she went, but then he crawled inside a bottle and refused to come out. Apparently he couldn't bear the guilt he felt at having been unable to save his own wife.'

Sally nodded her understanding. 'Grief and guilt can have very unpredictable consequences, and logic doesn't seem to have any effect on them.'

They were silent for a while, each absorbed in their own thoughts. But it was a comfortable silence, and Sally marvelled that the first friend she had made should be the self-contained, abrasive paramedic who'd made her blood nearly boil with anger the first time they'd met.

'What made you become a paramedic?' she asked, suddenly realising that she knew very little about him and that she wanted to know.

The strident ring of the telephone prevented him from answering.

'Dr Webster,' Sally said as she lifted the receiver.

'RTA,' the voice on the other end of the line said crisply. 'One trapped in the vehicle.'

Out of the corner of her eye she saw Luke straighten out of his chair as she repeated the directions to the scene of the accident. By the time she replaced the receiver he had their jackets in one hand and her keys in the other.

'Grab your bag. I'll drive,' he announced, already striding towards the front door before Sally could catch her breath.

'Hey!' Her indignant voice followed him across to the car as she locked the front door behind Amber. 'Who said you were coming with me? It's my—'

'I know the way. We'll get there faster.' His logical

words ended the argument instantly, and she climbed swiftly into the passenger seat.

Within seconds they were belted up and on their way, Luke's deft driving taking them rapidly through the outskirts of the town and out onto the more rural lanes.

Far from travelling silently, he treated her to a running commentary of the route they were taking and the directions in which each turning they crossed would lead. His knowledge of the area was almost encyclopaedic, and she let him know how impressed she was.

'The first chap I was sent out with was a local man who'd known the area all his life.' Luke gave a brief laugh. 'I once joked that he probably knew the names of all the people living in the houses we were passing, and with a perfectly straight face he said that he could probably tell you who all their relatives were and where they lived too!'

Their laughter died as they arrived at the scene of the crash.

The police were already there, their flashing blue lights lending everything a surreal air.

By the time Sally was leaping out of her vehicle they were being joined by the red lights of a fire engine, the crew racing to unload their cutting gear to release the trapped passenger.

The sight which met their eyes was horrendous—a small family saloon mangled almost beyond recognition under the wheels of a heavy quarry lorry.

'There's a pregnant woman trapped in the car,' the senior police officer began his briefing. 'Her legs are bleeding badly, and I've no idea how long it's going to take to get her out. We can't drive the lorry off without killing her, but by the time we dismantle the car around her she could be dead. . .'

Sally had been jogging towards the scene of the impact as he was speaking, and she raised one hand to show she had understood what he was saying before she ducked through to the car.

'What's her name?' she demanded of the group at large.

'Pamela Littlejohn,' an anguished voice supplied, and Sally spared a rapid glance for the bloodstained man who'd spoken.

'Pamela or Pam?' she demanded crisply, the tenor of her voice seeming to snap him out of himself for a moment.

'Pam,' he confirmed, in a stronger voice. 'She's six months pregnant.' He wavered for a minute, then drew strength from Luke's arrival with a blanket.

'Pam?' She reached out a gloved hand to touch the woman reassuringly. 'Can you hear me, Pam? I'm a doctor. . .'

Sally dismissed the poor man from her mind, knowing he was in good hands, and concentrated on setting up a very fast IV line, opening it wide to run saline in as rapidly as she could to minimise fluid loss.

Floodlights had been set up now, and as she tried to determine the extent of the trapped woman's injuries it almost looked as if the front of the car was awash with blood.

'Pam? Are you still with me?' Sally was leaning in through the shattered side window as she tried to determine the source of all the blood. She was frustrated that she couldn't get any closer until the fire crew could cut away the passenger door, but didn't dare move aside to allow them to get to work until she found out the nature and extent of her injuries.

'My baby. . .' the poor woman murmured brokenly.

'Save my baby. . .' And her hand fluttered over the taut mound of her belly.

'Can you feel your baby?' Sally asked as she placed her own hand next to Pam's. 'Do you know if it's a boy or a girl?'

She watched the woman's painful attempt at a smile before she spoke.

'Didn't want. . .to know,' she gasped. 'Like opening. . .presents. . .before Christmas. . .'

Sally felt a hefty kick against her hand, and smiled down at Pam.

'Well, if that's anything to go by, it's either a footballer or a clog-dancer,' she joked.

It was quite an effort to keep her professional smile in place when she peeled the blood-soaked hem of Pam's glass-strewn skirt up to reveal the extent of her injuries, and she rapidly reached one-handed into her open bag to grab a package of sterile gauze. She ripped it open with her teeth, not daring to lift her other hand from the wound she had revealed until she could replace it with a pressure pad.

'Sally?' Luke's voice reached her from the other side of the car, and she backed out of the vehicle just far enough to speak to him over the crumpled roof.

'Luke, I need more pressure pads and a tourniquet. Her femur's broken, and one end has punctured her thigh. She's in a hell of a mess, and we'll lose her if we can't stop the blood loss.'

'Coming up,' she heard as she ducked her head back inside and tried to decide how best to apply the last-ditch resort of a tourniquet.

'They want you out of there while they take the roof off.' Luke's deep voice came from a point close to her shoulder.

'Can't,' she said shortly. 'They'll have to do it round

me.' She was concentrating on threading the end of a triangular bandage under the poor woman's thigh, trying to get it as close as possible to the top of her leg. 'They don't want to risk—'

'Tell them to get a move on,' she snapped. 'Get the damned thing off before we lose her. I can't leave her now.'

She felt his hand on her shoulder, and the brief squeeze he gave her put new determination into her efforts.

'Got it,' she muttered as she placed a pressure pad under the broad, flat band of bandage, checking carefully to make sure that it would create pressure in the right position to slow down the flow of blood to the femoral artery.

'Here.' Luke's hand appeared over her shoulder with a pencil just as she was about to ask for one, and she began to twist it to tighten the tourniquet around the woman's thigh.

'Bleeding's slowing,' she announced after a moment. 'Can you note the time for me?'

'Done,' he confirmed. 'Have you got a hand free?' He passed a folded blanket into the car. 'Can you drape this over your heads? The remaining windows are going to go when they cut the struts.'

The next few minutes were filled with a terrible cacophony as the fire crew used their specialist cutting equipment to sever the struts holding the roof of the car in position.

With each cut Sally's ribs were jolted by the frame of the door, but she managed to maintain direct pressure over the puncture wound which had been created when the femur had broken.

There was a final tearing screech as the roof of the car was levered back against the lorry, and Luke removed the blanket covering the two of them.

'The parcel shelf has been shunted back against her lower legs,' Sally pointed out. 'If they can lever it out of the way without doing any further damage, or release her seat from its moorings so it can be shifted back, then we can get her out. Either way, they've got to hurry. She's lost too much to give us any leeway.'

She heard Luke relay her message as she scrambled in awkwardly over the side of the car. It was essential that she maintain pressure on the wound, but she also had to get Pam ready to be moved.

By the time the fire crew had managed to free her, by releasing the passenger seat and lifting it right out, Luke had provided essential assistance, so that Pam had been stabilised with a neck-brace.

With Luke taking over the job of monitoring the tourniquet and pressure pad, Sally had finally managed to tape dressings over the worst of Pam's injuries.

'How's the baby?' he murmured softly as his ambulance service colleagues took over to load her into the waiting vehicle.

'Still kicking, so far. . .' She pressed her lips together, her brows drawn down into a worried frown. 'I hope I managed to get enough saline going into her to last until they can get her matched. She's lost so much. . .' She turned to retrieve her bag and collect up anything that needed special disposal.

'Pam! Oh, God, Pam!' The distraught husband had just caught sight of his wife being loaded into the ambulance and ran towards her. 'I'm sorry, love. God, I'm so sorry. . .' he sobbed, and fought as a policeman tried to stop him getting in the way.

'Officer?' Luke stepped forward. 'If I may?' Sally watched as he put his arm around the man's shoulders and led him a short way away, talking all the time.

'Just give them a minute to get her in,' Sally heard him say calmly. 'As soon as they're ready for you they'll tell you, and you can travel with her.'

'Really?' He was hanging on Luke's every word. 'I can go with her?'

'Of course you can. She'll need you to hold her hand.'

'God, it's all my fault,' he wailed. 'I fell asleep at the wheel. . .I didn't even see the lorry until his horn woke me up. . .too late. . .too late. . .' He shook his head. 'I've killed her,' he sobbed. 'I've killed Pam and the baby. . .'

'Rubbish,' Luke broke in, giving him a shake. 'That baby's kicking up a storm in there. You wait and see.'

His head came up as the ambulancemen said they were ready to go. 'In you go,' Luke said as he led him to the steps. 'You hold her hand and talk to her. Tell her the baby's fine. . .' He stepped back as his role of comforter was taken over by his on-duty colleague.

'What happened to the poor lorry driver?' Sally suddenly realised that she hadn't even seen the man.

'He was very shocked, but otherwise unharmed. His cab was high enough off the road to escape most of the impact, and those lorries are very well reinforced.'

'Doctor?' It was the senior police officer again, his hand held out. 'You're the new volunteer on our patch, are you?'

'Guilty.' Sally smiled tiredly and gave a huge yawn. 'Oh! I'm so sorry.' She covered her mouth as it was followed by a second one.

'Too much excitement and not enough sleep?' he suggested with an understanding smile. 'I won't hold you up. We're bound to see each other again.' And he turned back to supervise the clearing of the road.

'What time is it?' Sally demanded round another

yawn. 'It feels as if tomorrow has come and I haven't had today's sleep.' She turned wearily to make her way back to her waiting vehicle.

'In you get.' Luke was there before her, holding open the passenger door and steadying her as she struggled her way inside without a hint of a complaint that he was taking over the driving again.

'Sally?' They were nearly back at her house before his voice broke the silence. 'Are you all right?'

'I'm a mess.' Her voice was disgusted. 'I gave myself a good shake before I got in, but I'm still covered in glass, and my fluorescent jacket looks as if I moonlight in a slaughterhouse.'

'Nothing that can't be easily solved,' he soothed as he reversed into position in her driveway. 'Stand on your front step while you take your outer clothes off, then it'll be easy to sweep up any glass. Your jacket only needs a rinse, and it'll be good as new.'

'All that depends on my finding the energy to do it,' she grumbled as she let her patient dog out for a mad five minutes in the back garden.

'Make me a cup of decaffeinated coffee and I might be persuaded to do it for you,' he offered, and Sally was too grateful to think of refusing.

By the time she'd taken the precaution of combing her hair for safety glass and the kettle had boiled, her fluorescent yellow jacket was once more hanging on the hook inside the front door.

'Coffee ready?' Luke's hopeful voice followed her into the kitchen as she put the two mugs on a small tray with a newly opened packet of biscuits.

'I thought we'd be more relaxed in the sitting-room.' She relinquished the tray into his hands. 'I haven't finished sorting it out yet, but at least I know that the settee is very comfortable.'

She led the way through, and drew a small coffee-table over for the tray.

'I see what you mean about sorting it out,' he laughed as he saw the results of her first attempt at paper-hanging.

'I've decided to use paint instead.' She pulled a face at the mess she'd made. 'It'll be quicker and cheaper in the long run—especially if Amber insists on helping with every piece.'

'Coward,' he taunted.

'Maybe. . .but I'd rather not end up with a giant jigsaw made up of the pieces of wallpaper she doesn't play with. At least with modern emulsion paints I can wash the walls down or give them another coat if I get tired of the colour.'

'And a few plants will give the room a bit of life,' he added as he looked round at the rather bleak décor.

'You and your plants,' she teased. 'Are you sure you wouldn't rather be an interior designer, or the owner of a plant nursery?'

They each deposited their coffee-mugs on the little table and sank back against the soft upholstery of the settee.

Sally had settled herself in her usual place at one end, her feet tucked under her as she leant back into the curve of the corner. Luke had sat himself right in the middle, one arm hooked up over the back of the settee so that he was angled towards her.

'I hope you don't take too many chances like that?' His voice rumbled in the silence, and she looked up from her contemplation of her failed decorating attempt to catch him frowning at her.

'Pardon?' She blinked, not following his train of thought.

'Draping yourself over the side of a car while it's being chopped up,' he clarified.

'Only when necessary,' she replied coolly. 'There didn't seem to be much point in allowing the fire crew to do it the easy way if it meant losing the patient.'

'Easy?' he choked. 'You could have been injured yourself—'

'But I wasn't,' she cut in. 'And mother and baby both stand a fighting chance.'

'OK—' he held both hands up '—I surrender. Just. . .be careful, won't you. . .?' His eyes had darkened, and as she watched him lean towards her she found herself holding her breath.

His hand lifted from the back of the settee to stroke the gleaming fall of chestnut hair she'd left to hang loose around her shoulders after its vigorous brushing to remove the glass.

'It's like silk,' he murmured, combing his fingers through it and allowing the strands to fall softly back into position.

A single sharp bark outside the back door reminded them suddenly that Amber was ready to come in, and Sally felt a moment's regret as he withdrew from her to allow her to uncurl herself from her corner.

'More coffee while I'm out there?' she offered, her voice slightly breathless with her unexpected reaction to his touch. 'Or is it too late? You'll need to get some sleep if you're on early shift tomorrow.'

'I don't sleep much, but no coffee for me, thanks.' He rested his head back against the upholstery and gazed up at her with slumbrous eyes. The knowing expression in their depths let her know that he was probably all too aware of her reaction to him.

Sally smiled in spite of her disappointment that their evening together would soon be over, and went through to let Amber in and lock the back door for the night.

She knew that she needed a few more minutes to regain control of herself before she rejoined him in the quiet intimacy of the sitting-room, and she paused to settle Amber on her bed, checking that the dog's water bowl was filled before finally pulling the kitchen door shut.

She turned to go back into the sitting-room, and almost bumped into Luke as he emerged into the small hallway.

'It's time I went,' he said quietly. 'Just because I don't sleep much, it's no reason to keep you awake.' He reached out to touch the shadows under her eyes, his expression sad and withdrawn.

'Don't push yourself too hard,' he cautioned as he reached the front door and turned back towards her. 'It doesn't make any difference in the long run—the fears and worries are still there waiting for you as soon as you stop. All you're doing is exhausting yourself. . .'

She gazed up at him, at dark eyes full of trouble that she could do nothing to help, and her heart was filled with compassion.

'Goodnight,' he murmured, and hesitated before he leant forward to brush her lips with his own. 'Sleep well.'

He straightened and turned the latch to let himself out, pulling the door closed behind him.

CHAPTER THREE

SALLY found herself thinking about Luke's words over and over again during the next few days.

As the frantic pace she had set herself began to take its toll she finally realised that he might be right. It wasn't until she drew up outside her house one evening and had no recollection of driving there that she knew it had to stop.

'Come on, Amber. Let's get you fed and we'll have an early night.' She held her door open for the patient animal to jump across her seat and then locked up.

She was just about to step up to the front door when she saw something standing on the mat.

'What on earth. . .?' Sally bent to part the paper wrappings, and saw the dark leaves of a plant. 'Luke,' she whispered with a chuckle, and her spirits rose.

She was still smiling when she carried it through to the kitchen and ripped the wrapping paper off.

'Oh,' she breathed as the plant was revealed in all its glory—the dark green of the succulent leaves a perfect foil for the delicate fuchsia-pink blossoms.

She was sure she should recognise it, but there seemed to be no label or instructions attached to the pot. She retrieved the paper wrappings to make sure the grower's instructions hadn't accidentally been thrown away.

With her past record it was quite possible that she'd have killed the poor thing by morning. The only person she knew who would know about such things was Luke, and, apart from the fact that he lived nearby, she had no idea how to contact him.

She could hardly phone the ambulance station to ask how to get in touch with him. For one thing, she couldn't be certain that the plant had come from him—even though she hoped it had.

More importantly, though, was the consideration of their reputations—there was no telling how fast the news would spread that she was trying to track him down, nor what interpretation people would put on it.

Sally resigned herself to having to wait for the next time she bumped into Luke to ask him about the plant, and was just about to crumple the paper up again when she saw the series of numbers written in one corner, their pattern telling her that it was a telephone number.

The only question was, whose number was it?

She walked across to the phone and sat down, a sharp excitement twisting her nerves in spite of her firm resolve as she tapped out the sequence.

'Hello?'

The familiar deep voice robbed her of breath for a few precious seconds, until she marshalled her scattered wits.

'What do I do with it?' she demanded in a husky voice, and was rewarded with a laugh.

'Good evening to you, too!' he chuckled. 'What do you think of it?'

'It's beautiful—you know it is—but I don't know what to do with it. The shop must have forgotten to put a care label on it.'

'It didn't come from a shop. It's a cutting from one of mine.'

'Oh.' Sally didn't know what to say. She'd never met anyone who knew how to take cuttings, let alone grow them into magnificent plants like the one sitting in the centre of her kitchen table. 'Well. . .' She gathered her thoughts together. 'The poor thing won't stand any kind of a chance if I haven't got any directions to follow at all. What is it?'

'Schlumbergera.'

'*Gesundheit*!' Sally giggled.

'That's Christmas cactus, to the ignorant.' She could hear that he was trying hard not to give in.

'But it's nearly Easter-time,' Sally objected.

Luke's slightly rusty-sounding laugh drifted down the line towards her. 'So? When you're a bit more confident, I'll tell you how to bring it into flower whenever you like—Christmas, Easter, in time for your birthday. . .'

'Not so fast,' she chuckled. 'First I need to find out if it's going to live.'

'It's easy.' His voice exuded confidence. 'Put it in good natural light—your kitchen table is in a good position by the window—and the tap water round here is fairly good, so you just have to give it a little to keep the compost moist.'

'There must be more to it than that.' Sally panicked. 'What do I do about the flowers?'

'Enjoy them,' Luke said simply. 'Just look at them and enjoy them.'

Each time she went into her kitchen Sally found herself remembering Luke's husky words.

He had been right about her kitchen needing plants to make it come alive. Even though she had little time to spend in her new home, she often found herself sitting at the table looking at the intricate design of the fragile flowers, marvelling at the glorious graduations in colour from the newest buds to the full-blown blossoms.

Somehow, knowing that his plant was waiting for her on her return home made the frantic pace of her days easier to bear—in spite of the fact that she hadn't caught as much as a glimpse of him in days.

Her own workload had unexpectedly grown lighter, with fewer patients booking in to see her during surgery hours.

It took a chance comment from one of the receptionists for her to realise what was really happening.

'Doctor?' Sue Lyons tapped on the door and stuck her head round. 'Ready for a coffee?' She pushed the door open and carried in a steaming cup.

'Wonderful.' Sally smiled at the friendly face. 'Have I got time before Mr Turton arrives?' She glanced at the next set of records on the pile.

'Well. . .' The senior receptionist paused, rather uncomfortably. 'Actually, he phoned to ask to see one of the other partners instead.'

'I see.' Sally's heart sank. 'Did he say why?'

'He said he wanted to see a "proper doctor".' She gave the words a touch of local flavour. 'Not one of these new-fangled lady doctors.'

'Good Lord.' Sally leant back in her chair with a thump, her forehead creased in thought. 'I know this isn't a big city practice, but I still wouldn't have thought you'd get much of that sort of attitude here. Is that why I'm getting off so lightly these days?'

'Well. . .' Sue screwed up her nose and glanced towards the half-open door.

Wordlessly, Sally signed for her to push the door shut and take the chair beside her desk, knowing that she could trust this mainstay of the whole practice to tell her the truth.

'What am I doing wrong?' she demanded in a worried voice. 'The rest of the practice aren't going to be very happy if they end up still carrying the load for one of the partners.'

'It's not really you,' Sue hastily confirmed. 'It's George. He was here so long that some of his patients feel disloyal when they come to you.'

'But he's retired!' Sally exclaimed. 'He wasn't fit to do the work any more—he'd started making mistakes.'

'We know it and George knows it—or he'd have fought retirement. Deep down, I think the patients know it too.'

'So what's the answer?' Sally picked up the pen she'd been using to make her notations on the previous patient's records and turned it end over end between her fingers, needing to focus on some physical activity while her stomach churned sickly. 'Would it be best if I offered to resign, so they could replace me with a male doctor?'

'Don't you dare,' Sue said stoutly. 'It probably wouldn't make an ounce of difference. He wouldn't be any better a doctor than you are, and probably much worse.'

'Thank you.' Sally acknowledged the compliment then returned to the existing problem. 'What *can* I do, then?'

'If you want my advice, just sit it out. You'll lose a few of the hardliners and bigots, but they'll be no great loss to you. People will gradually come to accept you for yourself—especially the women, and those with children. Eventually you'll look back on this time as the calm before the storm, when it's you they're all clamouring to see.'

'Oh, Sue, you're good for my ego,' Sally laughed.

'Well, I've seen it all before,' Sue said as she stood up and started towards the door. 'Each one of the doctors here had their own teething troubles when they first came.' She smiled as she reached the door. 'Take the opportunity to enjoy your coffee. I'll buzz you when your next one arrives.'

As she opened the door they both became aware of a sudden commotion in the reception area.

'Help me! Somebody help me!' a woman's voice was wailing, and Sue took off at a run.

Sally was halfway across the room towards the door when it was flung wide open and the noise burst in on her.

'Doctor! Help me. . . Help my Tina!' The distraught woman carried a swaddled bundle in her arms. 'She climbed in the bath and the water was too hot. . .' She flipped back one corner of the dripping towels to reveal a tiny lobster-coloured leg.

Sally reached across to punch the coded emergency button on her phone, knowing that an ambulance would be on its way within moments.

Guiding the poor woman swiftly to the examination couch, she gave her shoulders a quick squeeze.

'How old is she, and how long was she in the water?'

Sally began unwrapping the cold sodden towels so that she could gauge the severity of the problem, her eyes and fingers automatically registering the child's vital signs.

'Two. She was two just last week.' The woman drew in a sobbing breath. 'She wasn't in there long. I promise you, it wasn't long. I heard her scream. . . Oh, God. . .!'

'What did you do when you took her out? Did she have any clothes on?'

As Sally continued to keep her talking by firing the essential questions at her she was reaching for the necessary sterile packs to set up an IV. The little blonde-haired angel hardly whimpered, her teeth tightly clenched as she shivered convulsively in shock.

'No, she'd taken them off. She's just learned how to put the plug in the bath, but she must have just turned the hot tap on. I didn't realise she'd gone in there 'till I heard her scream. . .'

'What did you do? Did you put cold water on her?' Sally demanded, as soon as she heard the quaver in the woman's voice. She opened another container of water gel to spread over the child's chubby little legs, horrified as ever by the layers of skin sloughing off the tender little body, the flesh mottled and red. . .

'I sat her in the bidet. I filled it with cold water and sat her in it, and soaked the towels in cold water.'

'Good,' Sally praised, making certain that she met the mother's eyes for a second, to reinforce her words. 'You did exactly the right thing.'

She was swathing the little girl in wet sterile dressings when she heard the siren announce the arrival of the ambulance outside.

There was the sound of running feet and suddenly Luke was there, depositing his bag on the edge of her desk.

'What have you got?' His eyes were already busily taking in what she was doing.

'Two-year-old female climbed into a bath of scalding water. Mother put her straight into cold water and wrapped her in cold wet towels to bring her here.'

'Why here? Why not go straight to the hospital?' he demanded, confirming her findings with his own check of the child's vital signs.

'I only live two doors away,' the poor mother sobbed. 'Should I have taken her to hospital instead? Oh, God, Tina, I'm sorry. . .'

'No.' Luke put his hand on her arm and gave it a little shake. 'If you live that close, you did the right thing.' He turned back to Sally. 'What have you done so far?'

'IV's up and running, and I used it for administering pain relief. Her pulse and respiration are elevated, but stable. I've plastered her in water gel and covered that with wet sterile dressings. As far as I can tell, it looks as if it's second-degree burns, but only ten per cent of body area involved. Her skin is hypersensitive to touch, and blanches on pressure, and the hairs on the skin are intact.'

'Thank God for small mercies,' Luke murmured as he bent down beside their little patient. 'Hello, sweetheart,' he said, stroking her tearstained cheek softly with the back of one finger. 'My name's Luke. Would you and your mummy like to come for a ride in my car?'

He scooped the pathetic bundle very gently into his arms and turned to walk swiftly out of the room, his partner following with their unused bags of equipment.

Sally drew a deep breath and started setting the room to rights, conscious that her hands were trembling in the aftermath of the emergency. It never ceased to amaze her how her training came to the fore when it was needed—almost as if it bypassed her emotions. It was only later, when it was all over, that the emotional response was released.

'Poor little scrap,' she murmured as she disposed of the syringe she'd used to administer the quick-acting painkiller.

'Sue?' She pressed the button on the intercom. 'Is my next patient waiting?'

'Yes. It's Mrs Porter, but I'm sure she won't mind waiting a minute if you want a quick break for a drink.

You didn't get more than a mouthful of that coffee.'

'No. Send her in,' Sally said, knowing she would rather keep working. 'You can sneak a cup of coffee in after she's gone.'

Each of her patients commented on the excitement, waving away Sally's apology for keeping them waiting. She was delighted to realise that although there was a degree of voyeurism in their interest, there was an underlying concern for the fact that one of their neighbours had been involved.

This was something that Sally hadn't come across during her training in a big city hospital, and she hadn't expected to find that the people in a smaller community regarded each other almost as an extended family.

'You wait,' Sue commented as she brought in the long-delayed cup of coffee. 'This will probably turn out to be the best thing that could have happened.'

'Sue!'

'I don't mean that callously—I mean for you,' Sue explained hastily. 'By the time the story has done the rounds of those who were here and those who weren't, it will have been embroidered so beautifully that you'll never recognise yourself with your halo and wings on!'

Sally laughed in disbelief.

'You wait and see.' Sue wagged a finger at her. 'This will probably be the last quiet day you have in this practice. You're going to be rushed off your feet from now on. . .'

When two of the patients booked to attend the surgery that afternoon failed to show up, Sally was inclined to dismiss Sue's prediction. But—she shrugged her shoulders philosophically—time would tell.

In the meantime, she was determined to ration her time more wisely. She still had her little house to finish organising, and now that the weather seemed to be improving it was probably time to think about doing something with the garden.

She stood by the window in her kitchen with the tea-towel still in her hand, halfway through washing up after a solitary meal. She was looking out at the barren wilderness that was her back garden and wondering what Luke had seen when he had stood here. Had he regretted its emptiness, or had he seen its potential for beauty?

As if her thoughts had conjured him out of nowhere, his face appeared on the other side of the window, with Amber leaping around him in crazy abandon.

Sally turned to open the door, hoping her expression hadn't mirrored the leap of delight her heart had taken as soon as she'd seen him.

'What brings you here?' she greeted him as Amber pushed him in the house ahead of her.

'Duty,' he said in a sombre tone, walking past her towards the kitchen table. 'I've come to make a health-check on one of my offspring.' And he sat himself at the table and pulled the plant he'd given her towards himself. 'Hello, beautiful,' he crooned as he turned it around and pinched off a couple of dead blooms. 'How's she treating you?'

He tilted his head to one side as if he was listening, then nodded solemnly. 'Clean bill of health,' he pronounced, his eyes gleaming the colour of fine whisky. 'Certificate of confirmation on payment of one cup of coffee.'

'Idiot!' Sally threw the teatowel at him. 'If you wanted a cup of coffee all you had to do was ask.'

'Please, Doctor.' He put his hand up. 'Please, may I have a cup of coffee?' He straightened up out of the chair and walked towards her. 'I'll even make it, if you want to finish putting things away.' He gestured towards her interrupted chores.

They took the tray through to the sitting-room again, Sally eager to show off her progress.

'I like that.' Luke stood in the centre and turned in a circle to admire the completed decorations. 'You were right about the paint. Now, all it needs. . .'

'Is some plants!' Sally finished for him, with a laugh as she sat herself in her usual corner.

'Now that you mention it. . .' Luke clicked his fingers together as though he'd just remembered something, and left the room.

Sally heard him open her front door then close it again, and his feet coming back towards the sitting-room.

'Oh, Luke!' she breathed as he appeared in the doorway with an armful of plants in a rainbow of stunning colours. 'They are absolutely. . .' She shook her head in defeat as he stood there smiling.

'Now, then.' He turned to look around the room again. 'Let's see where each of you are going to be happiest.'

In just a few minutes he had placed the plants in groups around the room—one to cascade down the side of a bookcase, one to fill a small empty alcove with eyecatching colour, and two small groups on the windowsill and mantlepiece. Each one of them was a different version of the plant in her kitchen, and the variety was breathtaking.

'Well?' He finally sat himself in the middle of the settee and picked up his coffee cup. 'What do you think?'

'I think they're wonderful,' she said, her eyes never leaving his face, loving the open pleasure which filled it as he surveyed the effect of his arrangement. 'You love growing things, don't you? You like taking care of plants *and* people—like little Tina today.'

They both smiled, knowing that the prognosis for the child was good. The scald hadn't been as severe as they'd initially feared, and would probably heal itself without scars within three weeks.

He was silent for a moment, his eyes capturing hers as he thought about her words.

'I think it's a case of loving life,' he said finally, reaching out a hand to capture one of hers. 'Apparently I came very close to death in the accident, and when I woke up it was as if I'd never existed before that moment.' He frowned, as if he was trying to find the right words for his thoughts. 'In a way, it's as if I've had to invent myself.'

'Invent yourself?' Sally was struck by the strange phrase.

'I had to find out what I liked and disliked, what I was good at. . .' He shrugged. 'I had no past to draw on.'

'So what made you decide to become a paramedic?'

'I didn't,' he contradicted wryly. 'When I finally accepted that it was unlikely that a blinding flash of revelation was going to give me my old life back again, I had to think of some way to earn my living.'

Sally nodded her understanding and he squeezed her hand, his eyes full of bleak memories from that time.

'After I was discharged, I started off as a ward orderly in the same hospital. Then. . .' He drew out the word, his tone making it sound like the equivalent of a drumroll. 'Then I found out about ambulance drivers!'

'What?' She laughed at his gleeful expression. 'What about ambulance drivers?'

'Ambulances are allowed to break the speed limit,

ignore traffic lights, disregard keep left and keep right signs. . .I don't remember what I was like as a teenager, but I loved it!'

'You're an adrenalin freak!' she accused him.

'Guilty,' he admitted, and laughed.

'So that's why you made a collection of driving licences, is it? So you could drive ambulances all over the world?'

'Partly.' He sobered. 'I was also hoping that my driving skill was something I'd used before, and that my photo might have found a match in some gigantic computer somewhere.' He shrugged. 'In a way, I was longing for some petty official to shout "Eureka" when he found two licences with the same photo and different names and accuse me of being a fraud. . .'

They were silent for a while as they sipped their coffees, Sally staying perfectly still in case Luke realised that he was still holding her hand and took his away. The only thing she wasn't sure of was whether she was holding his hand for his benefit or her own.

'If you enjoyed the driving so much—' she finally voiced her thoughts '—why did you change tack?'

'I found out that I was even better at the medical side of things, so I took the courses and spent my two years "on the streets" before I was recommended to go for paramedic training. . .I seem to have a good instinct for it or something. . .' He raised one shoulder dismissively, but Sally knew what he was talking about.

In the few weeks since she'd joined Abbey Surgery she'd heard quite a few stories about 'lucky' Luke Nemo, and his almost uncanny knack of being in the right place at the right time with the right piece of equipment.

'Do you think. . .?' Sally began tentatively, only to

have Amber prance into the sitting-room to demand attention.

'She's a lovely dog,' Luke complimented her as she gazed adoringly up at him while he stroked her silky ears. 'How long have you had her?'

Sally calculated back to the day she had fled from Brian, believing her heart was broken. She had driven for hours until, by sheer coincidence, she'd parked in a remote spot and had found Amber trapped in barbed wire by a makeshift leash. She'd been pitifully thin and unkempt, and so terribly wary of any man that Sally was sure she'd been mistreated.

'Just under two months,' she said, amazed that it had been so long, yet unable to remember clearly what it had been like before she'd taken Amber on.

'Only two months? She behaves as if you've always belonged to her.'

Sally laughed at the way he'd phrased it, and told him the story.

'Bastards,' he spat. 'How could anyone mistreat a helpless creature?'

Sally smiled spontaneously, then laughed aloud, realising just why Amber was so taken with Luke, in spite of the fact he was a man. 'Luke Nemo, you *are* a fraud,' she accused him. 'You go around with a granite face to cover the fact that you're pure marshmallow inside!'

'Shh!' He put his hand over her mouth and looked around wildly, as though afraid someone might be listening. 'Don't let my secret out or I'll never live it down. . .'

His eyes were laughing down into hers as they clowned together, then suddenly the laughter died, replaced by a darker gleam as desire erupted in an instant.

As she gazed up at him she watched his pupils dilate, and felt the teasing hold he had on her face soften into the beginnings of a caress.

Amber, too, was aware of the tension which had sprung up between them, and it was her uncertain whine which broke the spell binding the two of them.

'What is it, girl?' Sally asked in a shaky voice. 'Did you want to go outside?' She uncurled her legs and planted her feet on the floor, not convinced that they would hold her if she were to try to stand.

She longed to look at Luke, to see if he was as stunned as she was by what had just happened, but didn't dare. She was afraid that her confusion would be obvious. . .

'If you wait here, I'll bring some more coffee in,' she mumbled over her shoulder as she fled.

The whole of the time she was in the kitchen she berated herself for being so cowardly. Nothing untoward had happened between them, so why had she scuttled away as if she'd done something to be ashamed of?

She admired Luke Nemo. Admired what he'd made of his life after waking up to a situation which would have destroyed most people. He was a fascinating, intelligent man, whom she found herself drawn to more strongly every time they met—not just physically, but emotionally as well.

Sally drew in a steadying breath and leant against the kitchen counter, gripping the edge tightly with both hands as she drew the inevitable conclusion.

After her betrayal by Brian, she had come to Abbey Surgery determined that she was going to be in sole charge of her destiny from now on. Her trust had been shattered in the most brutal way, and she'd sworn that no man would find his way through the armour she was placing round her heart.

Amber's polite bark outside the door drew her back to the kitchen, and she reached over to let her in, locking up carefully behind her and settling her for the night.

Her stomach churned as she put two fresh cups of coffee on the small tray and straightened her shoulders.

One thing she had learnt about herself in the last two months was that she had greater reserves of strength inside than she had ever realised. She was going to go back into the sitting-room and confront Luke. She was going to sit down and tell him about the situation which had resulted in her moving to this part of the country. She was going to tell him that, in spite of her fears and reservations, she was attracted to him. . .

Sally paused in the open doorway of the sitting-room, the quivering surface of the coffee demonstrating just how tightly strung her nerves were as she prepared to face Luke. She drew in a quick breath and stepped over the threshold, her eyes immediately drawn towards Luke.

A wry smile crossed her face as she took in the sight which met her eyes.

Luke Nemo was fast asleep on her settee.

His head was propped on the arm at an awkward-looking angle and his long legs were dangling over the side, as ungainly as a newborn colt.

'Oh, Luke. . .' she murmured with a smile as she saw how endearing he looked, with his face relaxed in sleep, his hair sticking out at all angles. There were the first faint traces of silver at his temples, but he looked younger, somehow. . .so much more innocent and open than the self-contained, wary man he was when he was awake.

She crept up to her airing cupboard and found a spare pillow and some blankets, and managed to settle them under and around him without disturbing his sleep. Even when she removed his shoes and lifted his feet up onto the settee he barely stirred, and she remembered him saying that he didn't sleep much.

Was that because he was one of those lucky people who didn't seem to need as much sleep as the rest, or was it because he found it difficult to find oblivion?

She turned the central light out, the small lamp in the corner throwing just enough light in his direction so that he could find his way if he woke up in the night.

'Goodnight,' she whispered as she hovered by the door, knowing she should leave him and go up to her own bed but knowing, too, that sleep would be hard to come by with Luke in her house.

CHAPTER FOUR

THE alarm woke Sally at seven, and she lay still for a moment in the early-morning silence, filled with the awareness that something was different.

'Luke. . .' she whispered into the half-decorated shambles of her room, and flung the bedclothes back, grabbing a handful of clothes on her way through to the bathroom.

The rich aroma of coffee met her as she sped down the bare wood of her stairs, and she found herself superstitiously crossing her fingers as she opened the kitchen door.

Amber looked up from her bed and thumped her tail in greeting, but otherwise the room was empty. It wasn't until she felt her heart sink that Sally realised how much she had been hoping that Luke would still be here. She would have loved to sit at the table with him and share a few moments of company while they drank that all-important first coffee of the day.

She turned towards the kitchen table with her favourite mug in her hand, and for the first time saw the note propped up against the plant pot in the centre.

Amber has been let out, and I made the coffee at six. I would rather have been woken by a kiss from the princess than her dog, but. . . Thank you.'

Sally frowned at his words, written in a distinctive scrawl, then laughed when she realised that Amber must have discovered that the kitchen door sometimes didn't close properly. She chuckled again at the mental image of Luke's reaction to an early-morning cold wet nose while rejoicing at the fact that he had apparently slept well right up till then.

She took her second cup of coffee through to the sitting-room and found a neatly folded pile of bedding on one end of the settee, the only sign that Luke had spent the night in the room.

The pillow she'd tucked under his sleeping head was on the top of the pile, and she found herself smoothing her hand over it as if she was some star-struck teenager.

'For heaven's sake,' Sally exclaimed in disgust as she walked briskly out to the kitchen again. She was a mature professional woman. What did she think she was doing, letting her hormones run riot while she touched the pillow Luke had slept on?

'Right, Amber,' she announced, reaching for an old waxed jacket and a pair of gloves. 'It's time to get to grips with the garden.' She laughed as the excited animal leapt around her, trying to steal the gloves out of her hand. 'Oi! None of that. I've only got half a day to get started. . .'

'Oh, no!' her shoulders slumped as the telephone shrilled imperatively. She'd really been looking forward to the physical exercise involved in starting to organise the garden. It would give her the chance to think about the direction her life was taking.

'Hello?' She'd padded across the floor in thick socks, her boots lying abandoned on the mat inside the door.

'Dr Webster? It's Sue. I'm sorry to ring on your morning off.'

'No problem,' Sally reassured her, and pulled a face at Amber, who had come back in from the garden and had flopped in a disgruntled heap just inside the door. 'What is it? A problem?'

'I've had a call from one of the patients on your list. She's bringing her daughter in. They're both distressed. Apparently the daughter's been kicked by a horse, and her head's cut and bleeding.'

'Good God.' The mental image was horrendous. 'Why isn't she taking her to Casualty?'

'Apparently the daughter's terrified of hospitals.'

'I'm on my way.'

Sally stepped on the toes of each sock in turn, to pull her feet out of them, and then rammed them into her well-worn trainers.

'Good girl, Amber. Come.' She swung the back door closed and pushed the bolt home, then set off towards the front door, grabbing her bag and jacket on the way. The good-natured animal was right behind her as she reached the vehicle, her tail up and her eyes alert as she leapt up onto the driver's seat and then down into her usual position in the footwell.

'Where is she?' Sally demanded as she ran into the reception area, her hand held out for the patient's record card.

'In One.' Sue pointed. 'Catch your breath. It's not nearly as urgent as we thought.'

'What?' Sally paused in mid-stride. 'You said she'd been kicked in the head. . .?'

'In a manner of speaking.' Sue grimaced and lowered her voice. 'Mother and daughter are well-matched when it comes to histrionics. Won't let nurse clean her up.'

'Ah, I see.' Sally nodded her understanding, and made her way along the corridor towards the examination room.

'Doctor!' As Sally entered the room she was accosted

by a cut-glass accent. 'Weren't you told that Saskia's been kicked? She's bleeding such a lot, and she's going to be terribly scarred.' The quiet sobbing in the background rose to a wail at her words.

'Good morning, Mrs Smith.' Sally looked up from her quick glance at the notes to see a woman thin to the point of scrawniness, her whole appearance determinedly youthful. 'Would you like to sit over here, please, so that I can have a look at Saskia?' She gestured towards the chair just inside the door, her voice raised over the sounds of distress.

'It's Armstrong-Smith.' The tone was decidedly chilly. 'And Saskia needs me over here. She's far too sensitive to have to go through this without her mother.' She sat herself back in the chair beside her daughter, and Sally got her first look at the patient.

One shoulder of the young teenager's pristine white jumper was liberally splattered with crimson, and her pale blonde hair was matted with blood all down one side. Her cheeks were marked by tear-tracks, but Sally noted that the china-blue eyes which matched her mother's showed little sign of real terror.

It was intelligence and keen interest which filled them as she looked from Sally to her mother round the edge of the dressing she was holding over the wound.

'Well, Mrs Armstrong-Smith, that leaves us with a bit of a problem.' Sally walked over to the sink and began to wash her hands.

'Problem?' the plummy voice challenged. 'Do you mean the injury is so serious that she needs a specialist?'

'No. Nothing like that. In fact, it's a very simple

job.' Sally plucked a fresh pair of disposable gloves out of the box and pulled them on with the ease of long practice. 'The only problem is that I need to be able to examine Saskia, and I can't do it if you're in the way. . .'

Sally paused as a slight movement behind the increasingly obnoxious woman drew her attention to the youngster's mischievous grin.

'Well, really. . .!' Mrs Armstrong-Smith huffed as she flounced across the room to the other chair.

'Right, Saskia. Let's have a look at you.' Sally moved over to stand in front of the youngster, and, gently peeling away the soiled dressing, she turned her head towards the light to inspect the damage. 'Hmm. It doesn't look as if you've been kicked. . .'

'I can assure you—' Mrs Armstrong-Smith started belligerently, but Sally totally ignored the attempted interruption.

'It looks as if one of the clenches might have risen, so that when the horse kicked out, the tip of the nail just nicked the skin.' Sally winked reassuringly at Saskia and squeezed her shoulder, receiving a surreptitious wink in return.

'First I need to clean you up a bit, then I'll give you something to stop it hurting while I tidy it up.' Sally glanced over the equipment which had been set out ready before Saskia's mother had sent the nurse out, and she prepared to irrigate the wound. 'Can you remember how long ago you had your last tetanus injection?'

'About four years ago, when I had to have stitches in my knee.'

'Good,' Sally murmured as she draped a towel around the slender shoulders and settled her in a comfortable position. 'One thing less to worry about,' she added as she concentrated on cleaning the wound and the surrounding area.

Sally kept half an eye on Saskia as she turned away to prepare the syringe, keeping it out of the youngster's line of sight as far as possible. She seemed to be very calm and adult about the whole thing—far more so than her mother—but there was no point in upsetting her unnecessarily.

'Is it going to hurt?' The small voice held the first trace of adolescent uncertainty, but Sally had no chance to reassure the youngster.

'Of course it will, darling,' Mrs Armstrong-Smith broke in, from just behind Sally's shoulder. 'The doctor's going to have to stitch it all together—' The words stopped abruptly as Sally whirled round to glare at her.

'Mrs Armstrong-Smith,' she said curtly. 'If you can't sit quietly without interfering, perhaps you'd better wait outside in the waiting-room.'

'Well, really!' She drew herself up indignantly to her full height, her bony face turning quite purple. 'How rude!' And she stormed towards the door, pausing as she reached it to fire a final salvo. 'It's a shame that Dr Lavenham isn't here. *He* knew how doctors ought to behave.'

Sally drew in an angry breath, and held it while she fought for control. She knew that she should have been more diplomatic, but the stupid woman was going to get her poor daughter all upset again if she carried on like that. . .

A smothered giggle beside her had her looking down at Saskia.

'She's been like that ever since Dad went off with his secretary. It's especially bad with anyone younger and prettier than she is. She really got you going, didn't she?' The china-blue eyes were wicked as they travelled from Sally's deliberately blank face to her hand.

'Oh, good Lord!' Sally raised the syringe for inspection and found that she must have clenched her hand unconsciously. The syringe was empty.

'Where did it go?'

'Up the wall!' Saskia pointed gleefully at the tell-tale arc of moisture across the pale paintwork, and giggled infectiously. 'It's the first time my mother's literally made someone go up the wall. . .!'

'All right, madam. Enough of this. We need to get you stitched up as quickly as possible.' Sally put on her sternest voice to hide the temptation to laugh, but Saskia seemed unimpressed.

'Why? So you can get rid of me as soon as possible?'

'What a good idea.' Sally turned away to get another phial of anaesthetic ready.

'No. I mean, really.' Saskia's voice was earnest. 'I'd like to know what you're going to do, and why you do it that way.'

'All right. I'll talk you through it while I'm working, if you really mean it.' Sally watched her carefully for any hint of squeamishness. 'If you start going green round the edges, I don't think your mother will be too pleased.'

Saskia giggled again, and pulled a face at Sally. 'Ow. That hurt.' She put her hand up towards the wound. 'Will it be a very bad scar?'

'Not if we get on with it.' Sally grabbed her hand to stop her touching the area she'd just cleaned. 'I started off by washing it thoroughly with sterile saline solution to help prevent infection—that's why you must keep your hand away.'

'OK.' Saskia settled back. 'What next?'

'Next I'll inject the anaesthetic into the tissues under and around the wound.'

'So I can't feel the needle going in when you're stitching, right?'

'And so that I don't hurt you while I'm checking the wound to make sure there isn't anything left in there. Also, I might have to clean up any ragged edges so that they'll repair cleanly.'

'What sort of stitches will you use? The ones that dissolve by themselves?'

'Not in this sort of wound. Those are for deep wounds. On a face-wound I use a fine monofilament, such as nylon or polypropylene.'

'How long will they have to stay in? A week?'

'Goodness, no. Only three to five days.'

Sally was finding it a strange experience, talking such a young patient through a procedure like this, but her obvious intelligence and interest almost made her forget her youth.

'As a general rule, the longer the stitches stay in, the more scarring they cause—and the more chance there is that they can become infected.'

She straightened up from her task and gave her handiwork a last careful inspection.

'Right.' She turned to deposit the tails of thread she'd just cut off, pleased with the neat result of her efforts. 'I'll just tape a dressing over this—'

'Can't I see it first?' Saskia interrupted. 'How many did you put in?'

'All right, you little ghoul. Slide down off the couch slowly, in case your legs are wobbly, and you can have a quick peep in the mirror on the back of the door through there.' Keeping her hands out of the way, she stuck her elbow out for Saskia to steady herself, but it wasn't really needed.

'Oh, wow! Four! Can I have them as souvenirs when you take them out?'

'I'll think about it,' Sally temporised. 'Now, sit down and let me finish off. I've got a dog and some gardening waiting for me.'

Sally managed to do an hour's work in the garden, but with Amber's over-eager assistance the results looked worse than when she'd started.

'Amber!' She threw her hands up in the air and conceded defeat when she saw the size of the hole which the dog was excavating, the plume of her tail waving ecstatically as she flung soil in all directions.

She'd already spread Sally's neat pile of dead leaves and branches all over the only patch of lawn.

'Come on, mutt. Inside. It's time I had a shower and got ready for work.' She rested her hands on her hips and looked up at the gorgeous spring day, sighing with regret for the fact that it would probably be dark by the time she finished work.

As she donned a smart pair of trousers and tucked the tails of an ivory silk shirt into the waistband she started to turn her mind towards the patients who were already booked to see her.

'Oh, Doctor, I'm so relieved.' The tearful woman was fighting to smile. 'I was so worried when I was waiting for the results—I nearly phoned to get you to tell me over the phone.'

'I can understand that.' Sally smiled. 'If I'm going to have a good cry I'd rather do it where I'm not going to have to walk out past a waiting-room full of nosey people.'

'I'm so glad I came.' The woman looked down at Sally's copy of the specialist's report in her hand. 'I never would have thought that it could have been. . . "sub-clinical mastitis",' she read the words out. 'It's been nearly fifteen years since I fed my youngest.'

'But you did have mastitis at the time, and the spring cleaning you've been doing recently must have upset things enough for the condition to flare up. How are you feeling now?'

'It's been a little easier since I stopped taking down the curtains and washing the paintwork,' she joked. 'That, and having the antibiotics the hospital prescribed. The lumpy feeling has almost gone, and so has the pain.'

'Good,' Sally encouraged, with a heartfelt smile. 'As you can see from the report, the fluid they aspirated was free of any signs of cancer—so it looks as if you've ended up with a cast-iron reason to get your husband to do all the heavy work for you!'

'I can't thank you enough for organising everything so quickly, Doctor. If I'd had to wait very long for the appointment I think I'd have gone round the bend.'

'No problem.' Sally retrieved the report and slid it in with the rest of the patient's notes. 'With your history, and the lumpectomy you had before, it was important to move quickly—just in case. But remember—' she paused to make sure she had the woman's entire attention '—I'd rather we had false alarms like this dozens of times than miss something important because you didn't want to bother me.'

'I understand.' Her nod was serious. 'I already know the benefit of early diagnosis from my first bout. I'm not likely to sit at home worrying about something until it's too late.'

After the door had closed behind her, Sally sat back for a moment and savoured her relief that a potential problem had turned out to be relatively harmless. The other major item in her reports pile hadn't been quite so encouraging, with a rare diagnosis of acute lymph-oblastic leukaemia for the pale young man she'd sent for tests.

He was already undergoing chemotherapy, to try to induce remission, but Sally knew that his age was against him. Statistically, his chances of success could be as little as sixty per cent, as opposed to the ninety per cent rate for younger patients.

The one thing she did know he had going for him was his absolute determination that he was going to beat it, and sometimes that could make all the difference in achieving success.

'Dr Webster?' Wendy's voice greeted her as she answered the buzz of the phone. 'Can you take a call before you see your next patient? It's a young girl, Emma Barber, and she insists on speaking to the doctor.'

'OK, Wendy, put her through.'

There was the usual series of clicks as Sue's deputy transferred the line.

'H'lo. . .?' The voice sounded very young and very frightened.

'Hello? Emma?' Sally answered. 'This is Dr Webster. What can I do for you?'

'It's not me. It's my mum and dad. They keep being very sick.'

'Can one of them come to the phone, Emma?'

'N-no,' the little voice quavered. 'I can't make them talk to me. . .'

Sally looked up as Wendy rapidly delivered two sets of notes, both in the name of Emma Barber.

'Listen, Emma. I need to ask you some questions?' Sally drew in a quick breath as she organised her ideas. 'Can you tell me how old you are?'

'I'm six on my next birthday. In Septober.'

Sally couldn't help the fleeting grin at the slip, but she needed one more item of information.

'Good. Now, tell me, do you know the number of your house, Emma?'

'Yes. It's 'leven Monk's Walk.'

'Clever girl!' Sally praised in a voice full of relief as she held up the notes that matched and Wendy disappeared to contact ambulance control and collect the notes for the child's parents. 'Can you do something for me, Emma?'

'What?'

'When I arrive at your house in a few minutes, will you open the door for me?'

'No. I mustn't.' The little voice was emphatic. 'My mum says I mustn't open the door 'less she says so. In case it's strangers.'

'Your mum's quite right. But this time she isn't well enough to tell you. . .' Sally shook her head in frustration. The child was perfectly correct to stick to what she'd been told. How could she be persuaded. . .?

'Emma?' Inspiration struck.

'Yes?'

'When I come to your house I'm going to talk to you through your front door. If you tell me something secret on the phone now, then when I tell you your secret through the door you'll know it's me.' Sally crossed her fingers, conscious that time was passing all too swiftly. 'Is that a good idea?'

'What secret?' The little girl sounded intrigued.

'Have you got an animal? A pet?'

'No.'

'What about a favourite toy? Do you take one of your toys to bed with you?'

'I've got my bestest dolly. . .'

'What do you call her?'

'Her name's Araminta,' she said proudly.

'Araminta?' Sally repeated, to make sure she'd heard correctly.

'Yes. She's got long yellow hair, just like mine.'

'So, when I come to your house and whisper to you that I've come to see Araminta, you'll know it's our secret and I've come to help your mum and dad?'

'OK,' said Emma, and the line went dead with a clatter.

'Make my apologies, Wendy,' Sally called as she grabbed the two case-records held out towards her on her way to the door. 'I'll contact you as soon as I know what's going on.'

The ambulance was just pulling up as Sally turned the corner into Monk's Walk. Sally's heart gave an undignified leap as she recognised the tall athletic figure of Luke Nemo as he ran swiftly towards the front door of number eleven.

'Luke. . .' she called softly across the intervening distance, before he had a chance to ring the bell. 'Hang on.' She grabbed her bag and ran across the grass and up the short pathway.

'What's the matter?' He had lowered his own voice in response to her quiet tone.

'There's a five-year-old the other side of the door, and she's been well-drilled in not letting strangers into the house.'

'Oh, Lord. What happens now?'

'Hopefully, we whisper the magic words.' Sally put her finger up to her lips to signal him to stay silent for a moment. 'Emma? Are you there?'

'Yes.' The little voice was developing a quiver, and Sally's heart went out to the brave little soul.

'Do you remember talking to me on the telephone a few minutes ago?'

'Are you the doctor lady?'

'Yes, Emma, I am,' Sally confirmed. 'Do you remember the secret you told me, so you would know it was safe to open the door?'

'Yes.'

'Have you got Araminta with you?'

'Yes.'

'Well, I've come to see Araminta. Will you open the door for me?' Sally crossed her fingers and glanced up at Luke's puzzled frown.

'That's our secret words, isn't it?' The stage whisper came to her at the level of the letterbox.

'That's right, Emma.'

There was a pause, and Sally was beginning to wonder whether Luke might have to break a window when there was a sharp click and the door slowly swung open just far enough for them to see that there was a kitchen chair in the way.

'Just a minute.' There was the sound of effort in her voice. 'I had to push a chair 'cos I can't reach. . .'

'Clever girl. Your mum and dad are going to be so proud of you.'

A worried little face appeared around the edge of the door, one arm clutched tightly around a pretty doll. 'They still won't talk to me. They're making funny noises and they're breathing all funny.'

'Can you show us where they are, sweetheart?' Luke had crouched down before he spoke, and Emma saw him for the first time.

'Who're you?' she demanded. 'You don't know our secret, do you?'

'I'm the doctor's friend. I've come to help her take care of your mum and dad.'

'Oh.' She nodded. 'OK.' And she turned and led them trustingly up the narrow stairs.

'Oh, my,' Sally breathed when they saw the mess on the tiny landing and in the cramped bathroom, and she drew the little child away as Luke prepared to check their two patients. 'Does this look like poisoning to you, too?' she murmured, so that the child couldn't hear.

Luke looked up at her as he checked their respiration, his brows furrowed in a frown as he nodded. 'Because Emma's unaffected, it's unlikely to be inhaled poison. It looks as if it's something only the two of them have eaten.'

'Emma.' Sally turned back towards the trusting child. 'When did they start feeling ill? Was it at breakfast-time?'

'No.' Her pretty blonde hair flew around her head like a wispy halo when she shook it. 'We went shopping, then we came home and had dinner.'

'Do you remember what you had for dinner?'

One part of her mind was on the questions she was asking, the other was on Luke's expert setting up of the two IVs—his colleague finding doorhandles and taps to suspend the bags of saline temporarily to leave their hands free.

'I had a chicken leg and some 'tato crisps.'

'Did your mum and dad have the same?'

'They had chicken, but Mum did 'tatoes in the microwave for her 'n Dad.'

'Why didn't you have potatoes with them?'

'Cos I don't like the skins.'

'Bullseye,' Luke muttered. 'Solanine poisoning from green potato skins. They've got all the symptoms—severe gastroenteritis, shock. . .'

'Thank God Emma called us before it got as far as apnea.' Sally deliberately used the clinical term, not wanting the child to know how close her parents had come to stopping breathing altogether.

'We'll load them in the ambulance and warn A and E what's happened.' Luke assisted Jeff in strapping Emma's mother into the carrying chair specially designed for manoeuvring in situations too narrow for a stretcher. 'By the time we arrive they'll have contacted the poison centre to confirm the best regimen to follow.'

While the two of them were being carried out and settled ready for their journey several neighbours came out of their houses to find out what was happening.

The woman living immediately across the road from Emma's family came running over as Sally appeared holding the little girl's hand.

'I'm Jane Thornton. My little girl goes to school with Emma. Is there anything I can do to help?'

'Do you know if Emma has any relatives in the area?' Sally was most concerned that there should be someone to take care of the brave youngster.

'Not as far as I know.' She shook her head. 'I can't remember hearing about any, and we spend a lot of time together.'

'So Emma knows your family well?'

'Oh, yes.' The smile forced its way through the worried expression. 'She spends as much time at my house as she does in her own. She's welcome to stay with us until John and Caroline are feeling better.'

'That would be wonderful. If you give me your address, I can phone you as soon as they're ready for her to visit. She'll want her mind put at rest about them as much as they will about her.' Sally released her hold on the little hand as Mrs Thornton swept Emma up into her arms. 'We'll have to make sure that her mum and dad know that she's a real hero.'

Out of the corner of her eye she saw Jeff close the doors at the back of the ambulance, shutting Luke in with his two patients, and she made her farewells to Emma and Mrs Thornton as she watched the vehicle set off in the direction of the hospital.

She set off towards the surgery again, but the feeling of satisfaction at a job well done was diluted by a lingering regret that she'd had no time to speak to Luke. They both led such busy lives that their meetings were fleeting, and usually fraught with responsibility for the lives of others.

It was so ironic, she mused as she finally drove home that night, that within weeks of escaping an impossible situation and vowing to have nothing more to do with men, she was busily trying to find ways of spending more time with one.

She reversed the powerful four-wheel-drive vehicle smoothly into her drive and switched off, slumping back in the seat tiredly. She still had a meal to cook for herself and Amber's needs to take care of before she could—

'Oh. . .!' She shrieked in surprise as the door opened beside her and a deep voice reached her out of the darkness.

'Are you going to sleep in here, or can I interest you in a home-cooked meal?'

'Luke! You scared me!' Both hands were pressed over the thunder of her heart while she tried to bring it under control. The only thing she couldn't decide was whether it was the shock she'd had which had made it beat so fast, or pleasure at seeing Luke again so soon.

'A home-cooked meal?' she echoed. 'Whose home, and who does the cooking?'

'"O, ye of little faith,"' he quoted. 'I'm wounded that you could even think such thoughts. I'm inviting you to my home, and the meal is already cooked. All it requires is your presence.'

'Would it spoil if I go inside for a few minutes to feed Amber and change my clothes? Sometimes, by the end of the day, I feel as if they're growing on me I've worn them so long.'

'No problem.' He stepped back to allow her to swing her legs round, then held her elbow to support her descent to the driveway.

The jolt which shot through her robbed her of breath, as if she'd touched a live power line, and as she slid towards the ground she wasn't really sure that her knees would lock firmly enough to hold her upright.

'Thanks,' she murmured breathlessly, conscious that her pulse was racing again as she turned to grab her bag and call Amber out.

She was still flustered when she stood under the spray of the shower, unwilling to put clean clothes on her sticky, tired body. As she towelled herself briskly she resisted the temptation to dress up for Luke's benefit, opting instead for comfort when she pulled on a loose sweatshirt over a clean pair of jeans.

'Ready?' he queried as she entered the kitchen. 'I gave Amber her supper while we waited for you.'

His voice was calm, almost nonchalant, but Sally had caught the flash of heat in his eyes when he'd watched her come in the room. Silently, stealthily, a faint flicker of warmth sprang to life in the corner of her heart that she had thought would stay frozen for ever.

'Ready,' she agreed as she reached for her jacket

and bag, suddenly conscious that this was the first time that Luke had allowed her to intrude on his territory.

Excitement tightened her nerves. Did this mean that he was starting to trust her enough to allow her inside the granite barriers that surrounded him?

She had a feeling that they had a lot in common, not just the skills they brought to their respective jobs—although they had proved in many ways that they worked well together.

There was so much they had to learn about each other, so much to share, which would result in a meeting of minds as they spoke of their hopes and fears, their successes and disappointments—the sort of sharing which could be the basis for a long-lasting relationship.

She took a deep breath and, realising how shaky she was feeling, held the keys out towards him.

'You can be chauffeur tonight.' She smiled. 'I'm in the mood to be pampered.'

'Your wish is my command,' He bowed elegantly as he plucked them out of her hand, his fingers brushing hers fleetingly to leave her tingling with renewed awareness. 'If madam would like to climb into her carriage, I will whisk her off to dine on nectar and ambrosia.' He opened the passenger door with a flourish, and bowed again.

Sally spoiled the gesture by giggling nervously, half afraid that he would touch her again, and that she'd disgrace herself by collapsing at his feet.

What an idiot! What a wimp! she railed at herself as he rounded the front of the vehicle. 'Behave yourself,' she muttered, only realising she'd spoken aloud when she caught sight of Amber's ears pricking up at her words.

This is just an invitation to share a meal, she reminded herself silently. Enjoy it and keep it in perspective. He hasn't invited you round to ravish you—more's the pity.

CHAPTER FIVE

'OH, LUKE. It's wonderful!' Sally stood in the centre of the room and turned round slowly. 'Did you do all this yourself?' She gestured at the ivory walls and saxe-blue curtains, and the upholstery accented with rich terracotta.

The whole décor was alive with dozens of plants grouped around the room—their pots, in shades of saxe-blue and terracotta, a beautiful foil for the deep green of the leaves and the flamboyant variety of the flowers.

'Yes.' His shrug was the picture of nonchalance, but Sally could see that her reaction had pleased him, and she hid her smile by walking over to the largest display of plants in a softly lit corner of the room.

'Are these all the same type of plant as the ones you gave me?' She bent forward to admire the subtle differences in the forms of the flowers.

'Most of them,' he agreed, and started to follow her across the room, only to be waylaid by Amber making her own tour of inspection. 'What's the matter, girl?' He crouched down to smooth his hand over her head and scratch her behind her ears.

'She doesn't know where you want her to settle,' Sally explained. 'It seems to be a hangover from her life before I found her. She waits to be told where she's allowed to lie down.'

'Well, that's easily sorted.' Luke straightened and clicked his fingers, leading the willing animal over to the deep terracotta rug in front of the unlit fire and pointing. 'Good girl, Amber. Sit.'

Without a second's hesitation she sat where he'd directed, and then flopped out full-length, as though grateful for the chance to rest.

Luke laughed as he looked back at Sally. 'You could almost hear her sigh of relief.'

'She's quite a ham. Loves playing up to an audience of children.' Sally smiled too, glad for the dog's presence to defuse the strange tension inside her.

'You said she's wary of men?'

'More than wary.' Sally nodded. 'In fact, you're the first one she's allowed to touch her since I've had her. You're honoured.'

'Well, you know what they say about dogs and children. You should always trust their judgement, because they're very hard to fool.'

Sally was just trying to think of a suitably flattening retort when her stomach rumbled loudly, her hunger aggravated by the wonderful smells drifting towards her from the open door of the kitchen.

'Don't you ever feed yourself, woman?' Luke accused her. 'Come and grab some cutlery while I serve everything out. We'll eat at the table I've hidden in the alcove off the kitchen.'

The meal was wonderful—succulent melon served with parma ham, followed by beef olives served with a selection of vegetables cooked just until they were still slightly crisp. By the time Sally had spooned up the last of her fresh fruit salad she was leaning back in her chair totally replete.

'Coffee?' Luke offered.

'I'd love some.' She groaned. 'The only problem is I don't know where to put it. I'm so full!'

'Good.' Luke stood up to collect the last of their dirty dishes. 'The way you push yourself, you need to make sure you refuel your engine.'

'Well, that was the best fuel my engine's had since. . .I don't know when.'

Sally dropped her eyes from the whisky-warmth of his as a memory flashed in front of her mental gaze. A memory of a delicious meal served in pleasant company that had left a bad taste in her mouth. She stood up from her seat at the table and reached for their empty glasses, needing to do something physical to dispel the awful feeling of loss, of betrayal.

'What?' Suddenly Luke was in front of her, his warm hand cupping her chin until their eyes met again. 'You've done that several times since we met. What is it?'

'Done what?' Sally stalled.

'You're talking and smiling, and suddenly you seem to remember something. . .something sad, and it's as if the sun goes behind a cloud.'

Sally shook her head, silently cursing his sharp eyes and uncanny intuition.

'You don't have to tell me.' He released his gentle hold on her, the tips of his fingers leaving her with a lingering stroke along the line of her jaw. 'But if you want to, I'm willing to listen.'

He turned back to finish clearing away, and Sally's eyes burned with the need to cry; not for Brian and the hurt he'd caused her, but for Luke and the tenderness he was offering.

'The same goes for you,' she murmured, in a voice made husky by her fight with tears.

Luke turned to face her, one eyebrow raised in query.

'You're probably in much the same boat as I am, with no one close enough to tell your troubles to,' Sally commented. 'We could make it a reciprocal arrangement—you listen to me and I'll listen to you?'

There was a long silence as they gazed at each other, and she was aware that he was measuring her words in some way. When he finally nodded she was flooded with a sense of relief that she'd apparently passed an important test.

'Why don't you go and sit on the settee?' Luke suggested. 'I'll just put the coffee on and finish loading the dishwasher.'

'Can't I do anything to help?'

'No,' he said firmly. 'You're being pampered tonight, remember? Go and make yourself comfortable.'

Sally sank into the deep upholstery of the saxe-blue settee, the terracotta shade of the nearby lamp casting a warm glow around her.

Amber had lifted her head, and her tail thumped lazily before she settled her nose between her paws and dozed again.

'I've put the coffee in a cafetière, so we can pour it when we're ready for it.' Luke arrived silently to deposit the tray on the polished wood of the circular coffee-table at his end of the settee, pushing one of the ubiquitous plants aside to make room.

As he sank back into the other corner of the settee he stretched luxuriously, crossing his long legs at the ankle and resting his head back against the squashy cushions.

Suddenly the situation seemed too intimate for Sally to cope with—the two of them relaxing together after a meal, with the dog on the mat by their feet. It was so much like the dreams she'd been nurturing—the dreams Brian had shattered, the dreams she'd banished for ever.

'All your plants. . .' She winced as she heard the

tension in her voice, but she couldn't bear to sit in silence. It felt too. . .too right. 'Are they really all from the same variety?'

'Most of them.' Luke glanced across at the group of plants she'd chosen to fix with her gaze. 'When I became interested in growing things, I decided to stick to flowering succulents.'

'Why?' Sally managed to croak out a rational question about his choice of plants when what she really wanted to know was why there seemed to be no air left for her to breathe when they sat this close. Why was her pulse beating so fast? Why was she so aware of the power and warmth of the body stretched out beside her?

'They're very forgiving if I'm a day or two late tending to them.'

Sally drew strength from his calm explanation, focusing on his words instead of on the scent of soap and virile male which seemed to surround her.

'In their natural habitat they sometimes get too much water and sometimes too little, so a minor variation at my hands doesn't seem to worry them. They still produce flowers for me.'

He leant across to pinch off a faded flower from the plant on the table beside her, his leg brushing hers and making her flinch away from the contact.

'I'm sorry.' He stiffened then drew his legs away so that there wouldn't be any possibility that they would touch. 'Are you ready for your coffee now?'

His voice was harsh, and Sally caught sight of the cold desolation of his face before he turned away. Suddenly she felt as if a knife had ripped through her, knowing that her involuntary reaction had been the cause of his withdrawal.

'Luke!' she cried impulsively, driven by compassion,

and he paused, turning slowly to face her.

'Yes?' His expression was so forbidding that she nearly lost the courage to speak.

'I'm sorry. I. . .' She shook her head, momentarily at a loss for words.

'It's not a problem.' He sighed. 'We can't be expected to control instinctive reactions. If you don't like people to invade your space—'

'No!' She leant towards him and reached out a hand to rest it on the tanned skin revealed by the sleeve he'd rolled up to load the dishwasher. 'You've misunderstood.'

'I don't think so.' He pulled his arm away until her hand dropped to the cushion, and made to turn again.

'It's the opposite,' Sally blurted, the words coming straight from her heart, bypassing the censorship of her brain, and she paused, horrified at the revelation.

She knew that a blush had swept over her face by the intense heat in her cheeks, and her eyes grew wider as the implications of her words dawned on her.

'Explain,' Luke ordered, his eyes fiercely fixed on her face.

'I. . . You. . . It's like electricity,' she stammered. 'I don't. . . I've never. . .' She shook her head, unable to find the words.

'Sally?' he murmured, drawing her gaze up from her contemplation of fingers clenched together until blue-grey met tawny. Silently he held out one hand towards her, and she found herself staring at it in fascination—the broad palm incised with lines, the fingers long and lean.

As she watched it started to tremble slightly, and her eyes flicked up to meet his.

'Luke?' she whispered uncertainly, mesmerised by the naked longing she saw in their depths. Almost of its own volition her hand reached out to meet his, and they grasped each other convulsively.

'Ah, Sally.' He gripped their joined hands with his other hand. 'It's the same for me. The electricity. But I don't even have to touch you to feel it.' He drew her hand up to his face and smoothed her knuckles against his jaw, closing his eyes as though to savour the sensation more fully.

'But you're so. . .' Sally shook her head helplessly. 'I haven't. . .haven't ever felt anything like this before. I don't know what's happening. . .or why.'

Luke was very still for a moment, then his eyes opened wide, the pupils so fully dilated that each iris was no more than a golden halo around the dark centre.

'You mean. . .you haven't felt sexual attraction before? You haven't wanted a man enough to. . .?'

Sally shook her head, unable to meet his gaze.

Unbelievably, Luke started to chuckle, and Sally reacted as if she'd been stung, pulling her hand out of his grasp. She was mortified, her cheeks blazing and her eyes hot with suppressed tears.

'Dammit, Luke,' she choked. 'I didn't think you'd make fun of me.' She struggled to rise from the suffocating softness of the settee, avoiding looking in his direction, as if he was some loathsome creature she'd found under a stone.

'Idiot.' Luke chuckled as he snared her arm, just as she regained her feet, and pulled her off-balance so that she fell against him.

'Luke!' She immediately fought to put some distance between them. 'Let me go.' Her breath was coming in sobs now, and she was horribly afraid that she wasn't going to get away before the threatening tears started to fall.

'No.' Luke wrapped both arms around her and tightened them until she was spreadeagled across his body, her clenched fists trapped against his chest. 'Not until you let me explain.'

'Explain what?' she demanded fiercely, in spite of her helpless position. 'Explain how you tricked me into revealing private secrets just so that you could laugh at me?' She bit her lip hard to still the quiver, knowing that tears were gathering along her eyelids.

'No,' he murmured softly, cradling the back of her head in one broad palm and pulling it down to nestle against his shoulder. 'I wasn't laughing at you. I was laughing at the situation.'

'What situation?' She still sounded belligerent, even though her face was buried against the warmth of his bare throat.

'It just struck me as ironic that we're both in the same position but for entirely different reasons.'

Sally thought hard, but she couldn't decipher what he meant. Perhaps it was because she was breathing in Luke's unique scent—a heady mixture of soap and man—that she didn't seem to be able to concentrate.

'What position?' she mumbled into the soft collar of his open shirt.

'For whatever reason, you've never been intimate with a man beyond a certain point.' He was obviously being careful about his choice of words. 'While I. . .' He paused, and Sally found herself holding her breath, knowing that if he continued she would learn something of the utmost importance.

She felt him shrug and draw in a swift breath, as though to brace himself.

'I seem to know all about it, as if I've been beyond that point, but I can't remember anything about it actually happening to me.'

For a moment Sally froze as she allowed the implications of his words to sink in. Gradually she became aware that Luke, too, was tense—almost as if he was waiting for a blow.

Suddenly the humour of it all struck her too, and she started to chuckle.

Within seconds the two of them were laughing helplessly, their arms wrapped around each other to prevent them falling on the floor. Amber joined in, whining and yipping as she tried to push her nose between them.

'It's. . .it's all right. . .Amber,' Sally gasped when she finally managed to draw breath. 'Good girl, sit. . .' And she lay bonelessly across Luke's chest, too exhausted to move.

'I'm sorry I hurt your feelings,' Luke murmured into the tumbled profusion of her hair. 'I should have explained. . .'

'How long is it since your accident?' Sally demanded, her brain finally clicking into action.

'Four years,' Luke said shortly. 'And before you ask—no, I haven't.'

Sally was silent. She could feel the renewed tension in the body she was lying across, and knew she had to wait until he was ready to speak.

'I haven't even wanted to,' he whispered softly. 'Not until I met you. . .'

Sally turned her head until she was able to see his face and found him looking down at her, his eyes full of confusion.

'Luke. . .' She brought one hand up to cradle his cheek in her palm. He covered her hand with his own and drew it far enough away to press a kiss in the centre, curling her fingers over the spot as though to trap the warmth in her hand.

His open vulnerability melted her last reservations, so that when he slowly angled his head towards hers there was no hesitation. She was waiting for him, her lips tingling with anticipation as he slanted his own over them.

It was like coming home. The dazed thought surfaced through the haze of pleasure as their lips met, parted, and met again, neither of them in any hurry.

For an aeon they explored—soft skin sliding, clinging and nibbling as they experimented with lips and tongues and teeth, first one then the other teasing and tantalising, until neither had breath to continue and they lay there tangled together and too exhausted to move.

Sally's head was pressed against the thunder of his heart, her lips tasting the throb of the pulse at his throat.

Slowly, gradually, breathing quietened, heartbeat steadied, and each of them gave a sigh, almost in unison.

'Wow!' Sally breathed, and felt the muscles in Luke's belly tighten as he chuckled.

'Now I know what I've been missing,' he whispered. 'It's much better than I imagined. . .' His words died away into silence and he gave her a hug.

Totally at peace for the first time in months, Sally relaxed, trusting Luke to hold her and keep her safe even as she started to fall asleep.

'Hey!' The gentle kiss on her forehead was accompanied by a shake. 'Wake up, Sleeping Beauty. It's time you took your poor dog home.'

Sally drifted back to consciousness to find Luke's tawny eyes gazing down at her, and she reached one hand up to the back of his head, running her fingers through his dark hair as she pulled him down to her for a gentle kiss.

'Thank you,' she whispered, and closed her eyes, knowing that her control was close to non-existent. If she were to look at him now he would be able to read the feelings she'd just discovered for herself—feelings of love so deep and endless that eternity wouldn't be long enough to explore them.

Halfway home, Sally drew in to the side of the road and switched the engine off.

She'd had an argument with Luke about driving home alone, but her emotions were still too raw for her to have stayed in his company any longer. She needed time to think. Time to come to terms with the discovery she'd made in his arms tonight.

The trembling in her hands had nearly gone, and she had just switched on the engine when the mobile phone rang, nearly making her jump out of her skin.

'Dr Webster,' she answered crisply, her free hand pressed over her racing heart.

'Accident in the multi-storey car park behind Market Square. One joyrider's trapped in the wreckage.' The male voice on the other end of the line gave the details crisply and concisely. 'Police, fire and ambulance have all been notified.'

'On my way,' Sally confirmed, sliding the gear lever into first even as she was replacing the telephone receiver. 'Hold tight, Amber,' she murmured as she pulled the vehicle into a tight turn. 'We're off to work again.' And she changed up smoothly, relishing the power at her command as she sped back towards the town.

At that time of night there was little traffic, and most vehicles were quick to move out of her way when they saw her flashing lights approaching in their rear-view mirrors.

A brief burst of her siren was enough to warn her colleagues that she was close, and she accelerated up the ramp leading to the parking bays to find a policeman ready to direct her.

The scene which met her eyes was something out of a horror film, and her foot hesitated briefly on the accelerator before she pulled up behind one of the police cars.

The strobe-like flashing of the blue warning lights made the steel-grey Mercedes appear quite ghostly in the darkness, and it wasn't until the police floodlights blazed out that Sally saw what a mess it was.

The driver must have been driving terribly fast to have misjudged the turn so badly, and he had hit the reinforced concrete wall so hard that the car had mounted the barrier and forced its way between the concrete and the steel rail above it, coming to rest with the front wheels suspended in mid-air from the top storey. Unfortunately, in the process, the roof had been flattened down almost to the level of the bottom of the windows.

'How many inside?' she demanded as she shrugged into her jacket and grabbed the handle of her bag.

'One. We got the other one out. He's injured, but not enough to stop him trying to do a runner.' The young WPC looked a little pinched and grey as she directed Sally towards her superior officer.

She hurriedly introduced herself, and found he was the same man she'd met when they'd been dealing with the pregnant woman.

'Where is he trapped?' Sally walked with him towards the damaged barrier, her eyes running over the buckled sides of the car to try and work out what she was up against.

'Driver's seat, we think. . . Because the roof's been crushed we can't see what position he's in.'

'Has anyone been able to check his vital signs yet?'

'We can't get close enough.' He directed her round to the passenger side. 'We managed to prise the back door open on the passenger side—that's how we got the first one out—but we can't get to the other one till we can release the car far enough to pull it back to safety.'

'That could be too late. If he's badly injured time is of the essence. . .'

For one brief second she registered that time was what she had hoped to gain by driving away from Luke tonight. Time to think.

For the young tearaway in the car in front of her, time could be running out.

'Can you get a chain on it?' Sally demanded as the senior fire officer joined them.

'What?' He blinked. 'Where? Why?'

'On the back of the car, to stabilise it.' She started shrugging out of her jacket, realising it would be too bulky to allow her to squeeze her way inside.

'Why?' he repeated.

'So that my weight won't send it right over the edge.'

'No. . .!'

'You can't. . .!'

The fire chief and the senior police officer both started speaking at once.

'Gentlemen!' She overrode both their voices. 'Thank you for your concern, but until I've had a chance to do my job you don't even know whether yours is worth doing and if you don't get a move on with that chain, I might be too late to do mine.'

She bent to select several packages from her bag while a fierce discussion broke out behind her, culminating in the sound of a heavy cable being positioned.

She straightened up in time to watch the winch tighten the cable around something underneath the car, and received a thumbs-up signal from the fire chief.

'Take it slowly.' An ambulanceman grasped her wrist for a moment. 'Don't take any unnecessary risks with your own life. . .'

Sally nodded, and stepped over the mixture of petrol and water that was seeping across the dusty grey concrete, the glaring lights picking out the rainbow iridescence. The fumes reached her and she wrinkled up her nose, longing to take a deep breath before she climbed inside the wreckage.

'Can you get everyone to keep the noise down while I'm in there? I'll need to listen for breathing. . .'

'No problem. . .'

The confirmation was the last thing she heard before she ducked down under the edge of the crumpled roof to slide full length along the smooth, expensive upholstery of the back seat.

'Can you hear me?' she asked, the question sounding unnaturally loud in the cramped space. 'I'm a doctor. Can you tell me your name?'

There was no reply. The only sounds she could hear were the ticking of cooling metal and the creaking of the winch cable as it adjusted to her weight.

Conscious that she had to keep movement to a minimum, she wriggled herself carefully around until she could reach between the two front seats, freezing in position for a second as she felt the car tilt, then settle.

Her hand found fabric, and she rubbed it between her gloved fingers to confirm that it wasn't part of the upholstery. She worked her way forward until she came to an arm and then found a hand.

'Any luck?' the ambulanceman called from outside, his voice sounding strangely hollow.

'I've found him. I've got his hand but I can't find his pulse. . .' Sally worked her way back along the arm she'd found, following it up towards the shoulder in the hope of finding a pulse in the neck. . .

'Oh, God. . .' She froze in horror. 'Oh, my God.' She withdrew her hand, and even in the poor light inside the ruined car she could see the darkness of blood. A great deal of blood.

'What is it? Do you need anything passing in to you?'

The ambulanceman's helpful voice hardly registered with Sally as she scrambled her way backwards out of the ruined vehicle. Her feet back on solid concrete, she straightened up, her hands clenched tightly into fists to disguise the tremors which threatened to shatter her like fragile glass.

'What is it, Doc? What did you find?' His hand squeezed her shoulder, bringing her to life again, to see the worried frown on his face.

'Tell them they can take their time with the car.' She gritted her teeth and drew in a steadying breath. 'It's too late for that one.' She gestured behind her with her thumb, not wanting to turn towards the vehicle, then concentrated fiercely on removing her gloves.

She didn't need to look at the car, didn't need to wait for the fire crew to retrieve the vehicle to see the evidence with her own eyes. Her imagination was supplying the picture transmitted by her sense of touch.

'Doc?' There was concern in the ambulanceman's voice. 'You look terrible. What did you find in there?'

'It was more a case of what I didn't find.' She swallowed hard at the memory, and shuddered as the bile rose in her throat. 'He'd been decapitated. . .'

'What a bloody waste of a life!' Sally railed in the darkness as she sat cradling a second mug of hot milk. Even a generous addition of brandy hadn't helped to relax her sufficiently to allow her to sleep.

Amber had done her best to comfort her mistress, curling up beside her on the forbidden territory of the settee with her head on Sally's lap.

Her fingers stroked the dog's silky fur, and she was grateful for her company. Reliving the ghastly events of the evening would have been so much worse if she'd been totally alone.

Not that she hadn't encountered death in many guises during her training—it was no respecter of age or station—but somehow this death struck her as the ultimate in pointlessness. A young man with his whole life ahead of him, and he'd thrown it away for the dubious thrill of an adrenalin high in a stolen car.

'What a waste. . .!' She drained the last of the milk and shuffled through to put the empty mug in the sink, the click of Amber's nails across the floor telling her that she was following close behind.

'I'm sorry to have kept you awake, girl.' She crouched down beside Amber's bed and stroked her. 'Thank you for putting up with me.' With a final pat she straightened up and made her way to bed, knowing that only exhaustion would let her sleep.

'So much for finding time to think,' she muttered as she thumped her pillow crossly then wrapped her arms around it and curled up on her side. 'At this time of night there's too much time to think, but none of the thoughts are worth having. . .'

She shifted about, trying to get comfortable enough

to relax, and remembered the comfort and security she'd felt in Luke's arms.

'If Luke were here I'd be able to sleep,' she mumbled crossly, remembering how easily she'd drifted off in his arms, her head pillowed on his chest with his heartbeat sounding reassuringly in her ear.

'Ha!' She gave a brief snort of laughter. 'If I had Luke Nemo here in bed with me, the last thing I'd be thinking about would be sleep. . .'

CHAPTER SIX

SURGERY the next morning seemed endless—especially after a broken night's sleep.

Several times Sally had woken, shuddering as she stared out into the darkness of her bedroom and relived her feelings as she'd tried to find the young man's pulse. . .

'Mrs Slateford.' She smiled as the next patient came into the room. 'What can I do for you?'

'I. . .I took one of those home tests and I think I'm pregnant.' The young woman's smile was tremulous with hope.

'Do you know how long it is since your last period?' Sally asked, smiling again.

'I've missed twice, now.'

'Well, let's have a quick look at you, then.' Sally came round from behind her desk to usher the woman onto the examining couch. 'If you slip your jacket off and push your sleeve up I'll check your blood pressure and take a blood sample to check for anaemia, then we'll weigh you.'

She kept up a soothing conversation, talking about the leaflets Mrs Slateford could collect on her way out, and suggesting some natural alternatives to control morning sickness when the young woman declined tablets.

'I'm not one of these women who'd risk their baby or their own health just to follow a fad, but I'd rather not take any medication if I can avoid it.'

'You'll probably need to take iron and folic acid to

keep up with the extra demands the pregnancy makes on your body.'

'Oh, I started to increase my intake of foods containing folic acid as soon as we decided to try for a family. We saw a programme on television that said it could almost guarantee that your baby wouldn't have spina bifida. . .'

Sally enjoyed the consultation. Mrs Slateford was an intelligent and well-read woman, whom she was sure would attend the antenatal clinics regularly. The prospect of a much-loved healthy baby on the way was one to gladden the heart of any doctor.

'You can phone the nurse in a couple of days, and she will be able to confirm your own diagnosis.' Sally smiled in response to the woman's happy giggle. 'She'll also be able to tell you the results of your blood test. If you do need a boost, I'll leave a prescription for you. In the meantime, it's just a matter of taking care of yourself and making sure you get enough sleep. The peace and quiet will soon be gone. . .'

She showed her out of the room and made a final notation on her record before calling the next patient through, her heart lighter than it had been all morning.

Sue handed her a message when she brought in her cup of coffee mid-morning.

'It was someone from the ambulance station. They want you to ring back about arranging a visit. . .'

At the mention of the ambulance station Sally's heart had leapt. She hoped it was a message from Luke. Practice policy meant that personal calls were only put through if the doctor was free. If there was a patient in the room, a message would be taken.

The piece of paper Sue had handed her just contained the number to ring, and the message she'd passed on sounded as impersonal as if it might be a standard get-to-know-you invitation to a new volunteer doctor.

She sighed and shrugged her shoulders, as though the prospect of seeing Luke in his work environment wasn't in the least bit interesting, and nonchalantly put the message slip to one side on her desk.

The façade cracked just as the door was pushed open by the next patient, and Sally grabbed the telephone number and slid it into the inner pocket of her purse.

At three o'clock the following afternoon Sally drew up in the visitors' bay outside the ambulance station and smoothed her hands over the knees of her favourite trousers to dry the nervous perspiration from her palms.

'Don't be so stupid,' she muttered to herself as she picked up her handbag. 'You're a qualified doctor and you're good at what you do. There's absolutely no reason to be nervous.' A little voice inside nudged her. But what if Luke's in there. . .?

Luke *was* there. In fact, he was the one who welcomed her as she pushed the door open, leading her through to the staffroom.

She followed him along the short corridor, helpless to prevent her eyes from devouring the lean beauty of his powerful body.

He held the door open and turned towards her to allow her to precede him into the room.

Sally dropped her eyes, but not quickly enough. In that brief second their eyes met, and she saw a searing flash of answering appreciation as he completed his own survey.

'We invited you along at this time because we're doing a shift-change,' Luke explained as she was offered a seat and a cup of coffee.

'This way you'll meet most of us in one fell swoop,' said his partner, Jeff, with a grin. 'An overdose of ambulancemen!' And he worked his way around the room, introducing her to everyone and telling her what their various jobs were.

Soon it was time for half of them to go off duty, and they left with friendly insults ringing in their ears.

'As soon as you've gone, we can tell her what you're really like,' called the young ambulanceman who'd spoken to her in the multi-storey car park the other night, and they all laughed at the threat.

Several of them accompanied her on her guided tour, and Sally found herself absurdly grateful for their presence. It helped to diffuse the awareness she felt every time Luke came near her.

There were several different ambulances drawn up in a gleaming row—from the traditional ones with the double doors at the back and room to stand upright inside to a specially converted saloon estate car capable of travelling at over one hundred and thirty miles an hour.

'Do you ever need that capability?' she questioned in amazement.

'Not often,' Luke conceded. 'But on a clear motorway with a very sick baby in the back it's wonderful to know just how fast you can get them to Great Ormond Street.'

Sally nodded, glad that the facility existed but equally glad that it wasn't her job to bear that type of responsibility.

'Do you have much problem with over-eager policemen?'

'Not once they realise what's just scrambled their radar,' young Terry laughed. 'Sometimes they take the registration number, and phone through to check that the vehicle *is* out on official business, but usually, as long as we're following all the safety guidelines, they let us get on with the job.'

They went back to the staff lounge to sit down, and Terry took a moment to speak to Sally alone.

'Are you OK after the other night?' he asked quietly. 'That sort of thing is enough to give anyone nightmares.'

'What was that?'

Sally didn't know Luke had returned until she heard his voice.

'The doc was called out the other night to that crash in the multi-storey—'

'The night before last?' Luke broke in, fixing Sally with a fierce tawny gaze.

'That's the one. The joyrider who wrote off the Mercedes.'

'And himself.' Sally shuddered.

'It was you—' Luke's words were bitten off, as if he didn't trust himself to continue, but his fierce gaze let her know that he would have more to say when they didn't have an audience.

For a moment Sally was intimidated by his anger, but then her shaky self-esteem emerged and she addressed the topic openly.

'In the event, my presence was a bit of a waste of time, as he was already dead, but if there's a chance—'

'A chance for you to kill yourself!' Luke exploded, startling everyone in the room with his vehemence.

'Luke. . .'

'No.' He rejected her interruption. 'You couldn't wait for the other rescue services to make it safe. You blithely crawled into a car soaked in petrol and hanging over the edge of a thirty-foot drop—'

'Luke!' She rapped his name out sharply, and the tirade stopped.

Into the uncomfortable silence Sally asked a simple question.

'If you'd been in my place, what would you have done? Would you have waited, knowing that the boy could have been bleeding to death, or would you have made the same decision I did?'

You could have heard a pin drop as a slow tide of colour washed up over the lean planes of Luke's cheeks.

'Probably,' he conceded in a rough voice. 'But—'

'But nothing,' Sally interrupted firmly. 'It's my job. I did what I'm paid for—' Her words were cut off by the strident tones of the telephone, and everyone turned to listen.

'Here we go,' Jeff muttered as he ran past her on his way out of the door.

Luke paused just long enough to speak to her.

'Can I call round tonight when I finish my shift?' His voice was urgent, as though her agreement was important to him. 'I need to see you. To speak to you. . .'

'You'll be seeing me sooner than that.' Sally grabbed his elbow and started to usher him out of the door. 'I'm on call too.' And she ran towards the familiar square outline of her vehicle without leaving him time to comment.

The fire was blazing fiercely by the time they reached the small industrial estate on the outskirts of the town, the furniture in the burning storage unit being a major factor in the speed with which it had spread.

Once again it was the fire crew at the forefront of things, their swift response to the situation helping to isolate the damage to just the one unit.

'Has everyone been accounted for?' Sally demanded when she ran the senior officer to ground. 'Have there been any injuries?'

'No injuries, as far as we know, but apparently someone in one of the units facing this one thought they saw someone going inside earlier on. It could have been one of the staff from the high street shop, coming to collect something for a customer—we're still checking.'

As he spoke there was a shout as a pane of glass shattered, shards flying outwards like deadly spears. All eyes went to the upper window, where the angry gleam of flames was now clearly visible.

'It'll really take hold now. The broken window is letting more air in to help it spread faster.' He shook his grizzled head. 'All we can do now is contain it. . .'

'Hey!' Sally's head swung round to the source of the shout. How had she known it was Luke's voice? 'There's someone up there.' He was pointing up towards the broken window.

Instantly there was a flurry of activity as the fire engine was rushed into position and the hydraulic platform raised to the level of the windowsill with two firemen aboard.

As one disappeared through the gaping hole wearing breathing apparatus it was like watching someone volunteering to visit hell, and Sally found herself holding her breath. Her pulse was racing in her ears as she tried to gauge how long he'd been inside—half of her wanting him to find someone, the other half doubting whether anyone could be left alive in there.

'Here he comes.' Luke's voice sounded in her ear, and she realised that she'd unconsciously walked towards him while her eyes were fixed aloft. 'He's found something.'

They both stepped forward as something was passed from one man to the other, just ahead of the flames now licking around the edges of the broken window. The hydraulic platform swung its burden to safety, one fireman cradling something in his arms.

'It's a child,' Sally gasped as they reached the ground, and she sped forward to intercept them.

The poor little lad was shaking and sobbing, his arms wrapped convulsively around a grubby scrap of blanket.

Before anyone could start to examine him a small car screeched to a halt behind the open ambulance.

'Andy!' a woman's voice shrieked. 'Where's my little boy? Oh, my God, where's Andrew?' And she ran towards the front of the furniture store.

'Mum!' their little patient croaked, and struggled to free himself from Luke's hold. 'Mummy. . .!'

His piercing cry cut through the deep roar and crackle of the conflagration, stopping his mother in her tracks before the firemen could catch her.

'Andy?' She whirled round, trying to locate the sobbing youngster. 'Andy, where are you?'

In spite of Luke's gentle attempts to hold him, Andrew struggled free and staggered to his feet, a ragged little urchin still clutching his comforter as he ran a wavering course towards his frantic mother.

Sally had to swallow a huge lump in her throat as she watched him being swung off his feet and cuddled tightly in his mother's arms, her voice alternately scolding and crooning to her miraculously safe son.

A policeman approached them and directed her to carry him over to the ambulance.

'We just need to check him over,' Luke explained

gently as he tried to persuade her to let go for a moment. 'Just to make sure he hasn't inhaled too much smoke and fumes from the furniture.'

While Sally and Luke checked her son's pulse and respiration the woman explained how she and her husband had come to the furniture store to choose a new suite for their sitting-room.

'My husband drove back to the shop to sort out the payment. I had to pay a visit to the toilet—we're expecting our second—so when the salesman drove me back in the van I thought Andy had already gone in the car with Bob.'

'I needed the toilet too,' a little voice intruded.

'It wasn't until I got to the shop that we realised we'd lost him, so I took the car to come back here.' She glanced over her shoulder at the horror behind her. 'I said when we were in there that I could smell smoke, but the salesman said they'd been burning a big pile of packaging materials earlier, somewhere out the back. . .'

She stopped her narrative as Luke straightened up.

'Is he going to be all right?' she said fearfully. 'You hear such terrible things about the dangers of cheap foam filling in furniture killing people with fumes. . .'

Luke shook his head reassuringly. 'I don't know how he did it, but your young man has come out of that—' he nodded at the fire '—with hardly a mark on him. He's been very lucky.'

'Does he need to go to hospital?' She had wrapped her arms around him as soon as Luke stood back, and was holding him tight, rocking him as if he was still a baby.

Luke glanced across at Sally with a questioning lift to one eyebrow.

'Probably not.' She smiled. 'I'll give his doctor a

call, to let him know what's happened, then if you're in the least bit worried about Andrew you can contact him and he'll know what's going on.'

Luke stood beside her as they watched her carry her son over to thank the firemen who'd rescued him.

'Definitely a case of all's well that ends well,' Luke murmured. 'I've no idea how he escaped so lightly.'

'No.' Sally shuddered. 'I can smell the smoke from here, and heaven alone knows how many different varieties of toxic fumes are mixed up in it. Why he isn't fighting for his life on a ventilator, I'll never know. . .' She paused as she became aware that Luke had gone very still.

'That's what they said about me,' he said roughly. 'Apparently I got this—' he pointed at the vicious scar that Sally no longer even noticed '—trying to get someone out of a burning car. The petrol tank exploded but, although I was knocked out and needed sewing back together, I was virtually unaffected.'

Apart from your memory, Sally thought sadly, knowing that his lack of knowledge of his past had probably done him far more damage than a physical injury.

As she drove back home to do battle again with the garden she found herself wondering what Luke had been like before the accident. Had he always been a quiet, self-contained sort of person, or had he once been the life and soul of every party?

She knew how gentle he could be from his dealings with the sick and injured people in the course of his job, but she also knew that he had a temper, and a very strong sense of right and wrong.

There were so many admirable traits to his character, she mused as she fought another tug of war with Amber over the dead vegetation she was trying to pile in a corner. Like his love of life in all its forms—plant, human and animal. . .

'Excluding one animal in particular, you wretch,' she panted breathlessly as she tried to catch Amber to retrieve one of her gardening gloves.

'Is this a private game, or can anyone join in?' Luke's laughing voice floated across the evening air.

Amber gave a sharp bark of welcome and abandoned the unwanted glove for more interesting game, prancing around him happily as he walked across the littered lawn towards Sally.

'It seems to be getting worse instead of better,' he teased as he paused to look around.

'Blame your furry friend.' Sally scowled darkly as she leant on her border fork. 'As fast as I tidy an area up, she either spreads all the rubbish right across the garden or she digs a hole in it.' She pointed out the series of excavations marring the freshly turned earth beside the lawn.

'Did you want some help?' Luke pulled his hands out of the back pockets of his jeans and offered to take the fork from her.

'I've had enough for today.' She blew a stream of air upwards, to try and remove the strands of hair straggling down onto her sticky face. 'It's time I gave Amber her meal and had a bath.' She bent to retrieve the small trug of tools at the edge of the path and deposited both gloves in it—one of them decidedly soggy.

'Can I make a suggestion?' Luke held out both hands for her burdens. 'You go up and have your bath while I organise Amber, then we can both sit down for a while.'

'You've no idea how tempting that sounds,' Sally sighed.

'Take advantage of it, then. The offer might never be repeated.' He smiled down at her, the last rays of evening sunlight turning his whisky eyes to pure gold.

'All right. I will.' Her heart lifted, and she returned his smile. 'I promise I won't be long.'

'Take as long as you like. Have a really good wallow. I could even come up and scrub your back for you.'

Sally could still feel the heat blazing in her cheeks as she lowered herself into the deep frothy water. She'd come so very close to agreeing with him, to inviting him up to join her in her bath. . .

It was less than half an hour before she came back downstairs to join Luke.

The bath had been wonderful; she didn't usually bother to pamper herself with perfume and foam, but it all paled in comparison to spending time in Luke's company.

'That was quick.' Luke glanced over his shoulder as he washed his hands at the sink, his eyes lingering on her as she paused just inside the door.

Suddenly she felt strangely shy of this big dark man who seemed so at home in her kitchen. She'd met him such a short time ago and they knew so little about each other. Was there a chance that they could both learn to overcome the problems that had made them who they were, or would they spend just long enough together for her heart to break when everything fell apart?

Amber's nightly ritual of chasing her dish around the floor brought Sally's attention back to the present.

'Thank you for feeding her for me. I thoroughly enjoyed my wallow.' She walked across to the kettle and lifted it to see if it needed filling. 'Can I offer you a drink?'

'Actually, I thought I might have earned a scratch

meal.' He took hold of her shoulders and turned her to face the view out of the window.

The warmth of his hands seeped through the brushed cotton of her shirt, scrambling her thought processes entirely, so that it was several seconds before she could see what he'd done.

'It's all tidy,' she gasped. 'You've managed to clear all Amber's rubbish away. How on earth did you persuade her to leave it alone?'

'By trickery,' he laughed, pulling her back to rest against his lean strength. 'Every time I threw her ball, she went to fetch it. And every time she brought it back to me, I threw it again.'

'Sneaky.' Sally laughed too, fighting her awareness of every inch where their bodies were touching. 'So she actually ended up more exhausted than you did?'

'And the rubbish stayed in a pile.' She felt his muscles tighten against her back as he laughed, and she stayed very still, just savouring the closeness.

'Ah, Sally,' he sighed, and she felt him rest his cheek on her hair, his hands sliding down her arms to clasp across her waist as he swayed slowly from side to side. 'You feel so good in my arms,' he whispered into the silence. 'I hadn't realised how much I needed physical contact. . .how much I needed this. . .'

In the reflection on the window Sally watched him tilt his head, watched as his lips slid softly down the curve of her cheek until they reached the angle of her jaw.

'So sweet,' he murmured as he captured the lobe of her ear between his teeth. 'So—'

The telephone burst into life beside them with a strident summons.

It rang three times before Sally's brain registered what she was supposed to do about the noise and she reached a shaky hand to pick up the receiver.

'Hello,' she croaked in a husky voice, then swallowed before she tried again. 'Dr Webster.'

'I'm sorry to call you out again, Doctor, but there's some trouble out beyond Abbey Meads. Possible gunshot wounds.'

'Where, exactly?' Sally's mind was suddenly functioning perfectly. 'And how many? I take it the police have been informed?'

'The first turning to the right after you pass the quarry turning on the left. About three-quarters of a mile. One of the policemen is a victim.'

'On my way,' she confirmed, and whirled round to walk straight into Luke. 'Oh! I'm sorry. I didn't realise you were there.' She made to go round him to get her bag and jacket.

'You're hell on my ego,' he said wryly as he held up her jacket and she realised that he was already wearing his own.

'I'm sorry about this.' She locked the back door and started towards the front of the house, picking up her bag on the way. 'One of the penalties of spending time with a doctor on call.'

She waited for Amber to follow them out of the front door before she locked that too, an alien heaviness in her heart at the sudden ending of their evening together.

'Perhaps you could come over when you next have an evening free?'

'Are you giving me the brush-off?' he said lightly. 'And after all that hard work I did in your garden, too!'

Sally looked across the bonnet of the car at him to find him waiting beside the passenger door.

'What—?' she began, her spirits suddenly rising like a hot air balloon.

'Come on, Doctor. Open the door. It's time we were on our way.'

Sally scrambled in swiftly and reached across to unlock the door, a silly grin reaching almost from ear to ear.

By the time Luke had settled his feet either side of Amber she had the engine running and her expression under control, and she clicked her seat belt in place before she emerged onto the road.

This time she knew where she was going, in spite of the fading light. It was only the last three-quarters of a mile down the narrow lane she hadn't travelled before.

'I don't know quite what I'm looking for,' she muttered aloud as she scanned the countryside over the hedges on either side. 'What would the police be doing out here, and how did one of them get—? Ah!' she exclaimed as she came over a rise and spotted a collection of ramshackle old buses and caravans. 'So-called "travellers", I presume.' And she pulled up behind a police car.

'Sally?' Luke's hand came out to cover hers on the brake and she looked up at him, her attention drawn by the strange note in his voice. 'Be careful. Please. . .?'

She gave a tremulous smile, then turned to jump down out of the vehicle.

'Officer?' she called as she retrieved her bag. 'I was told you had an injured man?'

'This way, Doctor.' He led her along in the shelter of the hedge before ducking down and sliding through a gateway. 'I'd keep your head down, if I was you. Tempers are very frayed at the moment.' He led her to the shelter of a second squad car, where a young officer was lying on the ground.

'What happened?' Sally knelt down beside him,

taking in the blood-soaked state of one side of his chest. 'How long ago did it happen, and do you know what sort of weapon it was?'

'Young fool got between the travellers and the farmer just as the farmer reached his limit. It was some sort of shotgun, but it wasn't at close range.'

There was an outburst of shouting, and the officer looked towards it then back at Sally.

'Will you be OK here with him, or do you need me to. . .?'

'You go and do what you're trained for.' Sally smiled at him fleetingly, hardly taking her eyes off the wound she was revealing as she cut away the blood-soaked uniform. 'We'll be fine here.'

The young policeman gasped as she peeled the tattered shirt fabric away from his chest and shoulder.

'I'm sorry to hurt you, but I must find out where all this blood is coming from,' Sally apologised, barely glancing away from her task as the noises on the other side of the hedge grew louder.

'Inside,' came the answer, through gritted teeth.

'Pardon?' Her hands stilled in their task.

'You said you were hurting me because you wanted to find out where all this blood was coming from. I thought if I told you, you could stop hurting me.'

For several seconds Sally gazed down at him in amazement, before she chuckled. 'With a sense of humour like that, you're obviously a survivor. What's your name?'

'William Hay. . .as in Will Hay—the comedian?'

'Oh, well.' Sally nodded her understanding with a straight face. 'If you got it through your genes, it's obviously not your fault.'

'Ha! Ouch!' young Will groaned. 'I like you. In

spite of the fact that you seem to be trying to finish off what the gun started.'

'You'll be pleased to hear that it's not a serious wound.' She sat back on her heels to extract a large sterile dressing from her bag and prepared to position it, working as quickly as she could before she completely lost all light.

'You couldn't tell that from my end of it,' he groaned. 'What damage has it done?'

'Mostly superficial,' Sally confirmed as she taped the edges of the dressing in position. 'You've collected a fair amount of shot in your upper chest and shoulder, but it hasn't caught any major blood vessels. When you get to hospital the nurses will have fun picking it all out of you. Within a few weeks you'll be able to tell your latest girlfriend that it's a war wound. . .'

'Or that a farmer blasted me when I was trying to raid his henhouse!'

Sally chuckled again, and set about packing her bag.

'If you'd like to sit up, you can lean back against the car to catch your breath.' Sally steadied him with an arm around his shoulders and positioned his ruined jacket to cushion him against the cold metal panel.

'As soon as you're ready, I'd like to get you to the ambulance. They'll be able to keep an eye on you until you can be transported to hospital.'

The journey back towards the place where she'd left her vehicle took a lot longer than the outward one as she combined steadying her patient and carrying her bag with crouching behind the shelter of the hedge.

When she finally handed him over to the care of Phil, one of the ambulancemen she'd met on her visit to the station, she was grateful finally to be able to straighten up.

The noisy confrontation was still going on between

the farmer who owned the land and the travellers, who wanted to appropriate one of his fields illegally.

The light had faded so far that Sally was unable to catch sight of Luke. There was no sign of his silhouette in her vehicle—in fact, she hadn't seen him at all since he'd held her hand and told her to be careful.

Bang! Bang!

The sound of both barrels of a shotgun being fired made them all jump. Sally's heart was racing with fear as she suddenly wondered where Luke had got to. Surely the police wouldn't have let him close enough to get between the protagonists, the way young Will had?

'I still don't really understand what it's all about,' Phil's voice drifted out to her as she sat on the top step at the back of the ambulance. 'The farmer isn't using that field at the moment, so what does it matter if these travellers camp there for a while? I know it's trespassing, but what harm can they really do?'

'Unfortunately, that's what a lot of people believe,' Sally answered quietly. 'They think the farmer's being greedy, or dog-in-the-manger. . .'

'Yeah,' Will agreed.

'What they don't understand is that the travellers have some, shall we say, less than hygienic habits, and it only needs one of them to contaminate the field with human waste and the farmer can't harvest any crops from it. Nor can he graze any animals in it—if he does, he can't send them to market because their meat could be contaminated.'

'Good Lord!' Phil sounded amazed. 'So if he lets them camp in his field, even for an hour, he could stand to lose thousands of pounds. . .'

'And that's not counting the damage to his gates and fences, and the disaster area they leave behind when they go.'

'I can see why the old man over there is fighting so hard for his rights.' Will's voice was subdued. 'If he's been hit by the recession the way some of them have round here, this could be enough to bankrupt him. . .'

There was a sudden commotion, with renewed shouting from several directions and the light of powerful torches waving about.

'I wish I knew what was going on out there,' Will grumbled.

'Hear, hear,' muttered Sally, desperate to know that Luke was safe but knowing it would be stupid to start wandering around in the dark looking for him. All she'd be likely to find was trouble.

The shouting rose to a crescendo, punctuated by an unearthly howl, and then there was a deathly silence that seemed to go on for ever.

Suddenly it was broken by the sound of engines being started, and as she peered through the ambulance and out of the front windscreen she could see headlights going on, and the tumbledown troop started moving away into the night.

'What's happening?' Sally demanded shakily, an awful sick feeling settling around her heart. 'Can you see what's going on?'

'They seem to be heading out as if the hounds of hell are at their heels.' Will was astounded. 'I've never seen anything like it. . .'

He paused as Phil drew in a sharp breath, and Sally suddenly saw what they had both caught sight of.

Two policemen were making their way towards the ambulance, supporting a third man between them.

'Another victim,' Phil confirmed, and Sally tightened her hand on her bag—prepared to help, whatever the injury.

There was the sound of a groan of pain as he was

half carried, half led round to the back of the ambulance, and Sally stepped down to leave the way clear for them to get up the steps.

They paused in front of her and the man made an effort to straighten up. The light from the back of the ambulance fell across the little tableau as Luke's tawny eyes gazed at her from a battered face and his arms wrapped around his ribs.

CHAPTER SEVEN

A WEEK later Sally would still feel sick when she remembered seeing Luke's injuries, but her first response was utterly primeval—a killing rage towards those who had done this to him.

'Oh, Luke,' she whispered, reaching out a shaking hand towards him. 'Your poor face. . .'

'Sally. . .' He tried to speak, but the croak which emerged had been painful to hear.

'Shh,' she soothed as she stepped aside to allow his human crutches to help him up inside the ambulance, following him as soon as they'd finished their task.

'What happened?' she demanded fiercely. '*How* did it happen? He's a paramedic, for heaven's sake, not a front-line policeman.'

'Try telling him that.' There was more than a touch of respect in the policeman's tone. 'Some of those beggars got hold of the farmer's old dog and started tormenting it. This idiot waded into them, and they set about him with fists, feet and anything else that came to hand. . .snivelling bunch of cowards.' His lip curled in disgust.

'That's why they took off the way they did,' his partner added. 'It gives them a chance to work out their lies among themselves and clean the blood off so we won't be able to pin it on the guilty ones.'

While they'd been talking Sally had directed Luke to sit on the side of the second stretcher, so that she could make her initial assessment.

'Why didn't you carry him in on a backboard?' Sally

demanded, her brain waking up from its initial paralysis. 'What if he'd had a spinal injury?'

'Stubborn beggar was already on his feet before we got to him, and ready to have another go at them,' one of the policemen said, with a degree of male approval.

'Idiot,' Sally snorted under her breath, and turned back to her examination.

Luke's breathing was slightly fast and shallow, and his pulse was rather rapid too, but she would check them again in five minutes to see if they'd stabilised. First, she was going to take a look at his head injuries.

'You're going to have a real shiner by tomorrow.' She tried to joke as she checked the grazed area over one cheekbone, her throat tight as she saw how fast it was swelling and realised just how close he had come to having his eyesight damaged.

'Look straight ahead for a minute,' she directed as she prepared to check his eyes for reaction to light.

His tawny eyes were dulled with pain, but each iris contracted normally as she shone the penlight across them.

'All clear,' she murmured reassuringly, and started to run her hands over his head and down his neck to check for any other bleeding or bumps and lumps.

It was so tempting, now that she had a legitimate reason to run her fingers through his hair, to savour the silky profusion of it between her fingers, but she resisted, her desire to make sure that he hadn't been badly injured by those mindless thugs taking precedence.

For a moment she was distracted by his scar, lightly tracing its jagged course from his temple almost to the crown of his head, and she suppressed a shudder at the severity of the injury that had robbed a man of his past.

Luke shifted uncomfortably, trying to sit a little straighter, and groaned at the pain his movement provoked.

'Where does it hurt? Your back? Your chest?' Sally slid his jacket off his shoulders as she fired the questions at him.

'Ribs,' he muttered, and wrapped an arm across his waist to clutch at his side as soon as she'd freed it from his sleeve.

'OK, let's take a quick look.' She reached for his shirt buttons and started to undo them.

His free hand moved convulsively, as if he wanted to stop her, but she glared at him and continued until she could slide the shirt down his arms.

Sally percussed both sides of his ribcage, taking extra care over the angry bruise on one side.

'No sign of pneumothorax or haemothorax,' she confirmed, with relief in her voice as she coiled her stethoscope away for a moment, 'but I think at least one rib is broken. We can wrap a pillow around you on that side, or strap your arm against it to ease your breathing, or you can hold your hand across it yourself.'

'Myself. . .' he muttered briefly.

'OK. You know what you'd prefer, but I want you lying down before they set off. Do you want oxygen before you move, or will you wait?'

'Wait. . .' he said through gritted teeth as he started to swing himself round.

'I'll support your weight while you lie down. Take it slowly. . .' She wrapped her arm around the naked breadth of his shoulders to minimise the strain on his ribs as he stretched out.

'I think. . .you'd better go,' he muttered laboriously, with a lopsided attempt at a smile for the waiting policemen. 'She's been dying to get. . .her hands on my body. . .for ages—' His words were finally cut off by the clear plastic mask of the oxygen supply.

The uniformed men were chuckling as they climbed out of the ambulance, as were their injured colleague and the ambulancemen on duty.

'No sympathy,' one of the officers called back over his shoulder. 'I've never had a pretty lady doctor around when I've been downed.'

'Luke,' Sally remonstrated in a strangled voice, knowing that her face must be scarlet. 'What on earth did you say that for?'

'You mean. . .it isn't true. . .? Ouch!' He'd tried to lift his head to follow her progress out of the ambulance, holding the mask away from his mouth to enable him to speak, when the pain caught him. Sally glanced back sharply, and saw him draw in several slow breaths before he relaxed again.

'We're going to need an X-ray of that, to find out exactly how much damage they've done, but I think you've come off fairly lightly.' She kept her voice crisp to cover her concern, but the expression on Luke's face told her that his brain was still functioning perfectly, even though his body was battered.

The gleam in his eyes, even though one lid was swollen almost shut, told her that he had registered her reaction to his injuries, and she was afraid that she wasn't going to be able to keep her feelings towards him secret for much longer.

'What am I going to do about him, Amber?' she asked her patient dog as she followed the ambulance back towards town. 'I don't know enough about him to be falling in love with him—hell, *he* doesn't know enough about *himself*. . .'

She pulled up in the hospital car park and fought

down the urge to rush inside to be with him. 'Come on, girl.' She held her door open and invited the dog to join her outside. 'You deserve to stretch your legs after sitting in there so long—even if it is only round a hospital car park.'

It was too close to Easter for the warmth of the day to have survived past the coming of darkness, and she was shivering by the time she finally allowed herself to approach the entrance to the accident department.

'Which consultant is on duty this evening?' she enquired when she reached the desk.

'It's Dr Scott, but she's with a patient at the moment, I'm afraid.' The motherly woman at the desk smiled kindly. 'If you could tell me what you wanted to see her about?'

'I just wanted to know. . .has she seen Mr Nemo yet? Do you know if he's ready to go home?'

'I'll just find out for you. . .' She went to turn away, then paused. 'Are you. . .? You're a doctor, aren't you?'

'Actually, yes.' For a moment Sally regretted leaving her identifying jacket in the vehicle, but she hadn't really come in an official capacity.

'I thought I recognised you.' Her smile grew broader. 'I was on duty when you came in with that young cyclist.'

'Oh. . .' Sally smiled distractedly. She didn't want to be rude to the friendly woman, but she needed to know how Luke was.

'You know your way around, do you? If you go through to Cubicle Three, Dr Scott might still be with him.'

Sally paused only long enough to thank her for directions before she was walking briskly in the direction she'd pointed.

The first thing she heard was the murmur of Luke's gruff voice, and she entered the brightly lit room to be confronted by his half-naked body stretched out in front of her.

The white adhesive tape supporting one side of his ribcage accentuated the lean muscularity of his torso, and contrasted starkly with the pale golden tan of his skin and the dark hair which spread between the dusky discs of his nipples.

'Hello, Sally.' Melanie Scott caught sight of her first, and her words had Luke's head turning sharply towards the doorway. 'What brings you here this evening?'

'What did you come here for?' Luke's words were less pleasantly spoken and caused a pang of hurt. He obviously resented her presence.

She raised her chin and focused on a point just past his ear.

'Unless Dr Scott is fitting you with wings or wheels in here, I'm your lift home. The bang on your head seems to have made you forget that you went out to that fiasco with me.'

'Oh. . .right.' He looked up at Melanie Scott. 'Am I free to go?'

'As soon as you like,' she confirmed, offering him her hand to help him up, then stepping aside as he rolled over unaided to ease himself onto his feet. She glanced across at Sally with a raised eyebrow, and they shared a wry smile at his determined independence.

'I'll send someone in to help you with your clothes—'

'No. . .thank you,' he interrupted hastily. 'I can manage.' And he turned away to retrieve his trousers.

It was Sally's first view of his back, and only her years of training prevented her from exclaiming in horror at the scarring across one side. She'd thought the scar on his head was bad, but the agony he must have endured while those burns healed. . .

'Sally?' Melanie's voice was right beside her, and she turned dazed eyes towards her. 'Would you like a coffee while you wait for him?'

'Y-yes. That would be nice,' she said weakly as she allowed herself to be led out of the room and along the corridor.

'You didn't know about that.' The words were more of a statement than a question.

'No. I didn't. . . We're not. . . We don't. . .' Sally stumbled to a halt, her face crimson.

'I'm sorry.' Melanie's hand rested briefly on her arm. 'I didn't mean to imply anything. I know he doesn't speak much about himself and what happened. How well *do* you know him?' Her gaze was forthright, and reminded Sally of a former headmistress of hers. She'd always seemed to expect to be told the truth too.

'We've met at several incidents and. . .and he's given me some plants for my house. He grew them himself,' she found herself adding with a smile.

'You care, don't you?' Melanie Scott said quietly. 'And he's let you get under his skin. I haven't seen that happen before. . .' She squeezed Sally's arm once, before she let it go. 'Good luck,' she whispered cryptically, and smiled as Luke joined them, leaving Sally frustrated that she couldn't correct her obvious misunderstanding of the real situation between the two of them.

'You didn't have to come to the hospital,' Luke growled as he settled himself stiffly into the passenger seat.

Sally noticed wryly that Amber had received a warmer greeting than she'd done, and closed the door beside him without speaking, resisting with difficulty the urge to slam it—hard.

She was in her own seat and reaching for the seat belt when he spoke again.

'I could have used one of the taxis from the rank in the hospital forecourt.'

'You could,' Sally agreed shortly, and started the engine, pulling out of the parking space as soon as she heard the click of Luke's seat belt.

It was an effort to pretend to be unaffected by his surly attitude—especially after her frantic concern for him and his injuries.

They travelled for several minutes before he broke the silence simmering between them.

'If you knew I could get myself home, why did you come for me?'

'Call it a result of an over-developed sense of responsibility.' She was finding it harder and harder to appear calm, but, knowing that his ragged temper was probably due to the fact that he had refused any pain relief, she made the effort.

'You're not responsible for me,' he argued.

'But I feel partly responsible for you being there in the first place.'

'B. . . Rubbish!' he denied hotly, only just managing to moderate his language. '*You* didn't try to beat me to a pulp.'

'No. But if you hadn't been with me when I took the call, you'd probably have been at home. . .re-potting your geraniums, or something.' Her tight control of the temper which had plagued her as a child slipped a little, and she made a violent motion with her free hand as she paused at a road junction, warning him not to interrupt.

'And it's not too late for me to try my hand at

beating you up if you carry on like this. I'll stand a good chance of success now that those animals have softened you up a bit for me!'

She reversed smartly into her drive, and switched off the engine.

'Now,' she said into the stunned silence which filled the air between them, 'you can get out under your own steam or I'll come round and help you out—it's your choice. Either way, you're coming inside with me for a meal.'

'But—'

'When you've eaten I'll drive you home.' She totally ignored his attempt to speak, and opened her door.

By the time she'd rounded the front of the car he had the passenger door open and was gingerly extricating his feet.

'Do you want help. . .?' She shook her head. 'No. Let me rephrase that. Do you *need* help?'

Luke fixed her with a stony glare, his face pale and glistening with a fine sheen of sweat as he sat hunched to one side, one foot in and one foot out of the footwell.

His sigh was audible.

'Yes. . .please. . .'

Sally supported him silently as he manoeuvred himself out of the vehicle while Amber sat in the driveway with her head on one side in obvious puzzlement.

'You can let yourself in the house while I lock up here.' She handed him the key and turned to get her bag out and check that the doors were locked, giving him time to regain his dignity. By the time she approached the front door he'd made his careful way up the path and had put the key in the lock.

'Do you want something to drink before I raid the fridge?' Sally offered, turning to hang her jacket up when she desperately wanted to help him take his off.

'A large whisky sounds about right.' He groaned as he twisted too far, trying to release his arm from his sleeve. 'But I'd better settle for coffee.'

'OK.' She started to walk towards the kitchen.

'Sally?' The soft word followed her, and stopped her in her tracks. 'I'm sorry. . .'

She turned slowly and saw the rueful expression on his face.

'It wasn't your fault, and I'm not being very. . .'

'Nice?' she suggested.

'I was going to say. . .fair. But you're right too.' He drew in a careful breath. 'I need some help with my jacket.' His voice was gruff, and heightened colour ran along his cheekbones.

Sally caught hold of his cuff and eased it off his hand. 'That sounded almost as painful as the ribs,' she teased. 'You're not used to asking for help, are you?'

'No,' he admitted as he followed her stiffly into the kitchen. 'I'm usually the one doing the helping. . .'

Sally made them each a quick omelette, keeping up a flow of light conversation as she watched him out of the corner of her eye.

'Damn,' he groaned, and squeezed his eyes shut as he tried to pull his chair up to the table, forgetting his taped ribs.

'Are you sure you don't want to take anything for the pain?' Sally offered. 'I've got. . .'

'No,' he bit out. 'No painkillers.' And he concentrated fiercely on his breathing.

'Don't you think that's taking machismo a little too far?' She struck out at him verbally, hating the helpless feeling of seeing him suffering and not being allowed to help.

'That's not why—' He shut his mouth, pressing his

lips together as though afraid to say too much.

'Tell me,' Sally coaxed, suddenly aware that this was something important—something she needed to know about the man Luke had become. 'Tell me why. I want. . .I *need* to understand.'

Eyes the colour of the whisky he'd refused to ask for delved deep into her own, as though he wanted to read her mind, her soul.

'It was. . .after the accident.' His eyes dropped to the omelette still steaming on the plate in front of him, his voice husky with painful memories. 'I was kept under sedation for some time—I don't really know how long. After I realised my memory was gone, it didn't seem to matter, somehow. . .'

He glanced up briefly, to find her gaze firmly on him—she couldn't tear it away—but there was no way he could know how tight her throat had grown, how hard she was having to fight the urge to go to him and wrap him in her arms.

'Anyway, I was on rather a lot of drugs for rather a long time, and I became. . .dependent. . .' He left the explanation unfinished, but Sally knew what he wasn't saying.

'If I promise to lock my bag away so you don't know where it is, and only give you a placebo instead of a real painkiller. . .'

His head came up sharply, his expression belligerent, as if he believed she was taunting him.

Sally saw his face change as he caught sight of the tears she'd been unable to prevent from spilling over.

He reached out one hand very slowly, and touched the silvery tracks with the tip of his finger.

'Why?' he whispered, shaken.

'Because you're in pain.' She swallowed, and tried to blink back the brimming tears.

He sat very still, his only movement the slight trembling of his fingertip on her cheek.

'It means that much to you?'

She pressed her lips together, unable to speak, and nodded wordlessly.

'Paracetamol,' he conceded quietly. 'And. . . thank you.'

They ate their meal almost in silence after that, but it wasn't an uncomfortable silence. It was strangely like the sense of peace after a violent storm, when the survivors were just grateful to be alive.

Somehow, the relationship between Luke and herself had changed. It was almost as if a bond had been forged between them—a sense of connection which she'd never known before. Not even with Brian.

She probed the thought as if it were a sore tooth, but the pain had disappeared. When had that happened? When had her broken heart mended? Or perhaps it had never really been broken at all. . .

A new sense of purpose filled Sally's life as Easter approached. Thc garden was slowly coming to life—new plants appearing out of apparently empty soil and fresh green leaves unfurling on every branch.

While Luke's ribs had been mending he'd spent time sowing seeds and transplanting seedlings for her—but only once he'd convinced her that he could manage to do it without jeopardising his recovery.

Hesitantly, she'd offered him a spare key, so that he had access to water and the key of her little toolshed, when he'd convinced her that he'd go mad unless he had something to do.

Several times she'd come home to the aroma of a home-cooked meal, and, with the surgery inundated with victims of a particularly contagious virus, she'd been more than grateful not to have to cook for herself.

The epidemic wasn't the only stress she was under at work, the senior partner finally having bowed to the inevitable and installed a computerised patient records system.

'I'm sure it'll save us a lot of time and effort in the long run,' she told Luke as they sat in the sitting-room after one of his delicious savoury concoctions.

Sally ran her fingers through her hair, her eyes closed wearily. She lifted the weight of the thick chestnut strands away from her neck in an attempt to relieve the pressure of the headache that had been threatening all afternoon.

'I've used them before, and it worked very smoothly, but until all the details have been transferred we're juggling between the old system and the new. . .'

She heard Luke shifting on the seat beside her and felt him take hold of her shoulders to turn her to face away from him. His fingers replaced her own, burrowing under her hair to massage the tight muscles.

'Oh, that feels so good. . .' She allowed her head to fall forward as he deepened the soothing contact, his thumbs working right up her neck to the base of her skull. 'I'll start purring soon,' she murmured as the tension gradually eased, leaving her deliciously relaxed.

'Better?' he murmured as he pulled her back to rest against him, her head settling naturally in the curve of his shoulder.

'Mmm. Much better. I feel quite dozy. . .' And she was unable to prevent her eyes closing, her limbs growing heavy. . .

'Sally. . .?'

Luke's voice came as a continuation of an enticing

dream, his arms were around her and his breath was warm against her cheek.

'Sally? It's time you went up to bed. . .' She felt him nuzzle her cheek, his own roughened by a tantalising day's growth of beard, and her dream suddenly became too realistic.

'Luke?' Her voice was slurred and sleepy. 'What are you doing in my bed. . .?'

He muttered something under his breath, and tightened his arms around her to help her sit up.

'You fell asleep on the settee.' He took his arms away and she felt chilled. 'You'd better get some proper sleep if you're going to do battle with the dreaded computer tomorrow.'

'Ohh,' she groaned. 'Did you have to remind me?' She leant forward to brace her elbows on her knees, her face buried in her hands. 'I was having a lovely dream. . .'

She finally woke up enough to censor her words, glad that her heated cheeks were hidden by her hands.

There was no way she could tell Luke that she'd been dreaming about him, about the two of them sleeping in her bed, with his arms warpped around her, and then being woken by his soft whisper in her ear. . .

'Sally?' His husky voice was insistent.

She jumped guiltily. It was almost as if he'd been reading her mind. . .

'Don't fall asleep again until you get into bed. You need your sleep. . .'

She dragged herself to her feet and walked with him to the door.

'I'm sorry I was such poor company,' she apologised. 'I hope I didn't snore. . .'

'No. Your manners were impeccable.' He smiled

down into her eyes, the hall light striking golden gleams between his thick dark lashes. 'You snuggled up against me like a sleepy kitten. . .' His words died away, his gaze sharpening, growing more intent as it travelled over her.

Strangely shy, Sally ran her fingers through her tumbled hair, conscious of her sleep-pinkened cheeks and rumpled clothing.

'Luke?' she whispered, mesmerised by his eyes.

'Ah, Sally.' He reached out to run the tips of his fingers down her cheek, then speared them through her hair to cradle her head in the broad palm of his hand.

Slowly, his eyes watching her reaction every inch of the way, he tilted her head back, his own lowering by degrees until their lips finally met.

Sally was only expecting a simple goodnight kiss—a token gesture of the friendship which had been building steadily between them the last few weeks—but *this* had nothing to do with friendship.

She watched his eyes lose their focus and start to close, his eyelids looking heavy and sleepy as he tilted his head to deepen the contact between them. Her own eyes closed, her concentration totally absorbed by the soft sweetness of his tongue as he traced the outline of her lips.

'Open your mouth for me, Sally.' The husky words were murmured against her lips, as if he couldn't bear to lose the contact between them. 'Let me taste you. . .'

When his lips opened over hers and the wet heat of his tongue probed at the joining of her own mouth she was powerless to resist.

With a helpless moan she opened for him, and felt her heart stop as his tongue met hers. A deeper groan resounded against her breasts, as though he was as stunned by the power of their reaction to each other as she was.

His arms tightened around her, pulling her into the strength of his body as he widened his stance, revealing fully the extent of his arousal.

For a moment she grew still, her mind fighting to assimilate all the information her body was sending, but it was too much—too much warmth, too much strength, too much need. . .

As if he heard her thoughts, he broke the kiss, pulling her head against his chest as he leant back against the wall. Under her ear she heard the thunder of his galloping heart and the ragged cadence of his breathing.

'I'm sorry,' he whispered, and her heart jolted with fear. She had been rejected once and the scars were still tender. . .'That got completely out of hand.'

'It. . .it's all right.' She squeezed her eyes tightly closed while she waited for the axe to fall.

'It's *not* all right,' he contradicted roughly. 'I don't have the right to kiss you like that. . .' His hands held her shoulders as he put her away from him. 'I must go.'

He reached for the door, his eyes avoiding hers as he stepped out and pulled it closed behind him.

Sally turned to watch him go, stunned by the speed with which he was leaving.

As the door closed without so much as a glance in her direction she leant back against the wall, where just a few seconds ago Luke had been leaning, and slid bonelessly down onto the floor.

Her arms cradled her knees and she stared blankly at the wall opposite, the taste of salt on her lips the first indication she had that she was crying silently.

Half an hour later she still wasn't sure why she was crying—was it the release of the anger and pain of

Brian's betrayal, or the heartwrenching uncertainty as to whether she had just been rejected again?

Luke returned to work just in time for the expected rush of accidents over the Easter break, and Sally was strangely relieved that he was likely to be too busy to call round for a while.

With the picture-perfect weather, life promised to be hectic.

Her own hours seemed unending, with the usual influx of patients overdoing the spring cleaning and decorating, or spending hours digging in the garden after a winter spent in an armchair.

'Why won't the idiots take it gently to start with?' Sally heard Gareth Evans' Welsh lilt complaining as she signed a batch of repeat prescriptions. 'If they didn't do their backs in, perhaps I'd have time to get out in *my* garden. . .'

She chuckled wryly as she went through to her own consulting-room, quite comforted by the fact that hearing this same complaint would probably become a regular part of her life as a GP. Each season would have its own focus for moans—with flu epidemics in winter and sunburn in summer only the more obvious ones.

As the only single doctor on the staff at the practice, she had volunteered at their regular practice meeting to provide back-up for the doctor on call.

'That's not fair,' Tony Hammond had objected. 'You could end up getting no time off at all—'

'Don't stop her,' Gareth had broken in quickly. 'I'm bloody shattered, and if she's willing to do it. . .'

'I am,' Sally had confirmed. 'You've all got families to spend time with—especially at a time like Easter. I'd just be kicking my heels.'

'You need to get a social life, my girl,' Tony had advised. 'You need something to take your mind off the job if you're going to stay sane.'

Sally had smiled, but she hadn't replied. She could hardly have said that, unlike them, she needed her work to keep her mind off her social life—such as it was.

Since Luke had walked out of her house without a backward glance she hadn't set eyes on him, and it was as if a gaping hole had opened up inside her.

Partly that was her doing, with surgery hours and home visits taking up huge chunks of her days, and trips out with Amber to learn her way about the region keeping her out of the house for all but essential sleeping time.

Thank goodness there had been a lull in emergency call-outs recently—her presence only required once, the crew on duty not Luke and Jeff.

It was only in the quiet of the night that she could admit to herself that she was exhausting herself for nothing. She was spending unnecessary hours driving around the district, on top of an increasingly heavy workload, just to avoid seeing Luke—when all she really wanted to do was spend time with him.

Finally, common sense prevailed, and she drove straight home at the end of surgery without any time-wasting detours. For the first time in days she actually reversed into her drive in daylight.

'Right, Amber. A quick change of clothes and a cup of tea, and we'll go out in the garden to see what's been coming up while we haven't been looking.'

Amber ignored her, busily chasing her bowl around the floor for that elusive final morsel.

Sally was just rinsing her cup when the phone rang, and for one awful moment her hand hovered over it.

What if the voice on the other end was Luke's?

'Dr Webster.' She made her voice crisp.

'There's a youngster trapped at the site for the new by-pass.'

'Which end of the by-pass, and do you know what sort of injuries?'

Sally blessed her reconnaissance trips; now she knew exactly how to reach the site as quickly as possible. She was less happy with the fact that there was almost no information about the youngster's injuries.

'On my way,' she confirmed, and called Amber as she put the receiver down.

'Wouldn't you know it?' she grumbled as she sped through the house. 'I finally decide to relax, and what happens?'

Amber panted happily and settled herself comfortably as Sally set off, oblivious to anything more than the fact that she was going out again with her beloved mistress.

Her arrival at the lunar landscape that marked the beginning of the new by-pass coincided with that of two fire-engines, and she realised that this was not a simple case of a child getting stuck while trying to break in to the site.

'Where is he?' she demanded as she sprinted across the rough terrain towards the tight knot of people, her bag almost an extension of her hand, she'd grabbed it so automatically.

'Through here, Doc,' called the familiar voice of the policeman she'd met twice before. 'We've got big trouble this time.'

As the wall of bodies parted to reveal a bright yellow vehicle lying on its side like a dying dinosaur she saw the top half of the young lad trapped beneath it.

CHAPTER EIGHT

'WHAT's his name?' She knelt down beside the young man, his nearly adult body seeming strangely childlike in its vulnerability.

Subconsciously she knew a fleeting gratitude for the fact that she was in her gardening clothes when the damp, sandy soil chilled her knees.

'Tim,' a voice behind her supplied.

'Hello, Tim. I'm a doctor. Can you tell me what happened?' Her eyes and hands were moving swiftly, collecting vital information even as she was preparing to administer oxygen.

'He was going to—' Sally glared in the direction of the helpful voice and hoped she would have a chance to explain later that it was important that *Tim* spoke, so that she could gauge his mental state.

'Tim?' she prompted. 'Can you tell me how you got in?'

She started a large-bore IV in the back of his hand, with an over-the-needle catheter, and set the saline as fast as it would flow.

'Hole in the fence. Protesters cut it. . .' He gasped as she tried to explore the extent of the injuries to his lower body; his legs were almost totally out of sight.

'All right, Tim.' She nodded as a blanket appeared over her shoulder, and hands draped it carefully into position.

As soon as she'd drawn off blood samples, ready for checking blood type and cross-matching, she turned towards the nearest official person she could see and held them out.

'Can you find someone who can get these sent back now? He's on saline at the moment, but we might need an immediate transfusion once he's released. If they can't supply a match for any reason, we'll need O negative or even plasma.'

She took hold of Tim's free hand and held it tight for a moment. 'I'm going to tell you what I've done so far, then I'll explain what I'm doing as I go along. You can ask any questions you like. OK?'

'Am I going to die?' Frightened blue eyes filled with tears as he whispered the words inside the plastic mask.

'Not if I can help it.' Sally's voice rang with determination as she monitored his blood pressure. 'The firemen are working around us to lift this monster off you, and then we'll get you out and on your way to hospital.'

'Will you have to cut my legs off?' A tear slid out of the corner of his eye and washed a clear track through the dust at his temple, finally disappearing into his sandy-coloured hair.

'I'd only do that if it was the only way to keep you alive.' Sally deliberately met his eyes as she spoke.

'Promise?' he whispered.

'I promise.'

'Sally?' An all-too-familiar voice behind her demanded her attention. 'They're ready to take the weight of the machine. If you could move out of the way. . .'

'Why?' Her pulse was beating far too fast for her to manage more than a single word. It was Luke's voice. Luke was standing right behind her. . .

'In case a cable slips and you're injured. . .' His

words were softly spoken and meant just for her ears.

Sally felt the convulsive movement in the arm under her hand, and her eyes flew to the young man's face. He had obviously heard what Luke had said too, and his eyes were wide open and full of desperation as he reached out to grasp her hand.

'Please. . .' She saw him mouth the word silently, his eyes speaking volumes about his fear of being left alone.

'Then they'd better make sure they get it right first time, hadn't they?' Sally said quietly as she gave the grubby hand a reassuring squeeze.

'Sally—' Luke began to remonstrate.

'Luke.' She cut him off, knowing what he was going to say and why. She couldn't allow him to dictate when she knew that she was right, but at least she could tell him why.

'When that thing's lifted off him, Tim will need rapid medical assistance. I won't be able to give it to him if I'm sitting on my bottom halfway across this bomb-site just to comply with safety regulations. For anyone suffering from crush syndrome there isn't a second to waste, so I'm *not* leaving him.'

She started to turn back towards Tim, then spoke to Luke again. 'Oh, while you're here, you might as well give me a hand with the cervical collar, and then you can go and tell them what I said.'

Luke's eyes bored into hers, his concern evident. He was silent as he helped her position the collar round Tim's neck until, finally, he nodded.

'I'll tell them,' he said softly as he rested his hand briefly on her shoulder in a gesture of understanding. 'As soon as the blood arrives and you're ready, I'll give them the signal to go.'

'What's crush syndrome?' Tim's voice interrupted

her thoughts as she watched Luke stride across towards the fire chief and the burly man in charge of the lifting equipment.

'It's something that happens when someone is trapped under wreckage of some kind,' Sally explained briefly, not certain exactly how much he wanted to know.

'In car crashes, you mean?'

'And under buildings, after explosions and earthquakes.'

'Does it mean all my bones have been crushed?' He sounded so fearful that Sally quickly explained further.

'No, it's more concerned with your muscles and the rest of your soft tissues. When they're squashed by a heavy weight it stops the circulation, so they can't get any fresh blood.'

'What does it do? Does it mean I'll get gangrene and have to have them chopped off anyway?'

'It means we'll have to get everything timed just right when they start lifting. Your tissues have been crushed and damaged, and when the weight is lifted off you'll lose a lot of blood into the tissues. If we time it right, we'll have the blood ready to transfuse immediately, so your kidneys will hardly realise that there was a problem.'

In the distance there was the familiar sound of a siren approaching at speed.

'That sounds like the blood coming now,' Sally commented as she made another series of observations and murmured the figures over her shoulder to the unseen figure who had volunteered to act as 'secretary'. 'We'll soon have you out of here at this rate.' She smiled down at Tim, trying to hide her concern at his condition.

His eyes had dulled and his colour, which hadn't

been good when she first saw him, was now almost non-existent.

'Come on, come on,' she muttered under her breath as frustration grew inside her. 'We need to get him out of here *now*, not this time next week. . .'

Running footsteps approached her, and Luke arrived with his hands full.

'We've got two units, matched, one of O neg and a plasma. As we're within fifteen minutes of the hospital they're having more transferred there, so it'll be waiting for him when he gets there.'

'Good.' Sally reached for the first unit and prepared it.

'I'll put a second line in his other hand and hook up just in case.' Luke suited his actions to his words, and once again Sally admired his speed and technique. Many doctors she knew would have loved to be able to perform that procedure as proficiently as he did.

Luke reached behind him and slid a backboard into position.

'As soon as they raise this thing enough to free his legs, we'll pull him straight out onto the board and get him clear. Jeff's standing by to lift with me, so you'll be free to monitor him.'

'But. . .' Sally's eyes flew to his; she was intending to refuse his assistance while the dangerous lifting manoeuvre was under way. Logically she knew that the process would need at least one more pair of hands, but she had discovered that she was just as protective of his safety as he was of hers.

She saw the steely determination darken his eyes and didn't bother voicing her objection, knowing there was no point. Once Luke had made up his mind. . .

'Are we ready?' Luke held her gaze for a long second as his eyes delved deep inside her, his presence giving her the mental sustenance she needed for the dangerous minutes ahead.

Sally glanced away on the pretext of checking Tim, shaken by the depth of emotion roused in her by a simple meeting of eyes that had quickly become far from simple.

'Ready,' she agreed huskily, and he turned his head to give the signal.

There was a discordant symphony of human shouts and mechanical groans and shrieks, but they were almost drowned out by the crescendo of sound as her heartbeat pounded frantically in her ears.

The first sign of movement was almost infinitesimal. If she hadn't been looking for it she would never have noticed the little trickle of loose soil tumbling away from the brightly painted metal of the excavator.

'It's moving,' she whispered, her eyes riveted to the spot, waiting for the next sign. 'Can you see it?'

'Yes. I can see it my side too,' Luke murmured, one hand mirroring hers as they each held the units of blood clear.

'They've taken up the slack.' Jeff's voice called from his position just beyond the scene of operations. 'Are you ready for them to go ahead?'

Sally looked across at Luke and found in his eyes the same mixture of apprehension and determination. He nodded at her with a small smile of understanding.

'We're ready,' he called back.

The sound of the heavy motors was louder now as they strained to contend with the inertia of such a huge machine.

Suddenly Tim gave a muffled cry, which rose to a scream as the behemoth rose up above them.

'Wait for it,' Luke cautioned as he monitored the

distance. 'Another couple of inches. . . Now!' he shouted, and they pulled together, sliding Tim's body out with one sustained effort so that he ended up on the backboard between them.

'Jeff!' he shouted, but his right-hand man was already running towards them as Sally and Luke quickly adjusted both IVs to run wide open.

'Got it,' Jeff panted. 'Let's get out of here.' And they lifted him between them and started to move swiftly away.

Sally had grabbed the second IV bag from Luke as soon as Jeff had arrived, and made certain that she kept pace with them until they were clear of the site.

'Down and secure,' Luke directed, and they stopped at the first piece of nearly level ground where Jeff had left the rest of their equipment. 'He needs splints on those legs—inflatable ones for speed. They'll help prevent him going into shock from the loss of blood into the crushed tissues.'

The three of them worked swiftly to stabilise Tim's legs before the two paramedics strapped him securely onto the backboard.

Sally held both bags up with one hand while she made a rapid check of Tim's vital signs. By the time she gave the signal that he was ready to move two other rescuers had arrived to help transport the injured man into the ambulance, and he was soon on his way to hospital.

Sally stood up and arched her back, conscious that she'd been hunched up in one position for far too long. She braced her fingers at her waist and rubbed the muscles either side of her spine with deep circular motions of her thumbs as she watched the flashing blue lights disappear in the distance, the sound of the siren taking a little longer to fade.

As always, there was that sense of anti-climax after the patient was on his way. She had done her best and now it was up to others to carry on with the job.

'Doc?'

She turned towards the voice and found the senior police officer walking towards her.

'What are his chances? Will he lose his legs?'

'I hope not. However stupid he's been, he doesn't deserve to have that happen. Was it just a prank that went wrong?' She stooped to retrieve her bag and gathered up the debris to take with her.

'From what we can gather from one of his mates, there were some holes left in the perimeter fencing after some environmentalists descended on us to try to stop the by-pass being built.'

'They obviously didn't succeed.' Sally looked at the scene surrounding them.

'No.' He laughed reminiscently. 'They got sent off with a flea in their ear by the locals. They've been *begging* for this road to be built for nearly twenty years.'

'So what was our young friend doing here today? A one-man rearguard action?'

'No, nothing like that. He was just taking advantage of the fact that the site was closed for the Easter break. He was hoping he could have several days of practice on that thing—' he pointed his thumb over his shoulder at the huge yellow machine '—without any of the locals realising he wasn't one of the normal crew.'

'He didn't really think he'd get away with it, did he? Is he mad?'

'Apparently he's *car* mad. Drives anything he can get his hands on—with or without the owner's permission. By all accounts he's a natural, and he desperately wants a job driving in some capacity, but at seventeen he's still got a few years to wait before anyone will take him on.'

'If he ends up with any legs,' Sally added sombrely.

'Well, it won't be for lack of trying on your part,' he said. 'You're getting to be a real asset around here since you moved into the area. You'll be keeping the paramedics on their toes. . .' He laughed.

Sally felt her cheeks grow warm and hoped he would think that the compliment had embarrassed her, rather than his reference to paramedics.

She made her farewells, knowing that she still had at least half an hour's work to do before she could collapse in a chair with a cup of coffee. *That* would have to wait until all her equipment had been checked and replenished, just in case she had another call-out.

Sally nearly went round to Luke's house that evening, her emotions in turmoil after the intensity of her reaction to him at the accident.

'What do you think, Amber?' she said as she cradled her mug between her hands. Her elbows were resting on the table as she gazed out at the gradual transformation of her once barren back garden.

'Should I go and see if he's off duty? Do you think he'd like to come to see how the plants are coming on before it gets dark? Perhaps I could persuade him to stay for a cup of coffee. . .or a meal?'

She chuckled to herself. 'God, I sound like a desperate spinster trying to hook a man. . .' She stood up to empty the dregs into the sink.

'Alternatively, I could have an early night—start off with a lovely relaxing bubble bath, with soft guitar music playing in the background, then curl up in bed with a romantic book until I fall asleep.'

She pulled a face as she checked that the doors

were locked and admitted to herself that her alternative scenario could just as easily have been a continuation of the first one. If she *had* invited Luke to come round, she'd have had company for the relaxing bubble bath and the soft music, and she'd have had no need of the novel at all. . .

'Oh, for those days when the patients didn't want to see me,' Sally moaned to Sue when she handed her a long list of home visits at the end of surgery. 'I actually had time to do gardening and decorating then. Since Easter, I don't even have time to breathe!'

'Far be it from me to say I told you so—but I told you so!' Sue laughed as Sally stuck her tongue out on her way past. 'See you tomorrow.'

'Not if I see you first,' Sally threatened, and made her way out to her car.

It was strange to climb in without a welcome from Amber, but after a couple of very long warm days she'd become worried that she wasn't being fair to the poor animal, keeping her cooped up in the car for hours at a time.

Today, she'd decided to detour past her own home to collect Amber before she set off on her visits. That way, her faithful shadow wouldn't miss out on the companionable part of the job.

The first call was from the parents of a five-year-old who'd just been to school for the first time.

'He's been ever so sick for several hours now,' his mother said, looking down at the pathetic little bundle curled up in his pyjamas and dressing-gown in the corner of the settee. 'He started almost as soon as he got home, and I thought it was just because he was a bit overtired or something.'

'Is he just being sick?' Sally sat down on the side of

the settee and smoothed her hand over a mop of silky fair hair almost as thick as thatch. 'Have you got any pains anywhere?'

She could feel that his temperature was raised considerably, as was his pulse-rate, and his chubby little face was pale and sweaty.

'My tummy,' he moaned softly. 'It hurts in my tummy.'

'Can I have a look at your tummy, to see if I can find out what's making it hurt?' Sally coaxed.

'I tried giving him some water, but he even brought that back up,' his mother said as she helped him to unfasten the buttons on his pyjama jacket and slide the diminutive trousers down to his non-existent hips.

'And you say he's just five?' Sally palpated the whole of his stomach area gently, including his groin. The only problem she found was the mass in the right side of his stomach.

'Owww,' he wailed as her fingers homed in on the painful area. 'That hurts!'

'I'm sorry, sweetheart,' Sally soothed. 'Just one more look. . .' She checked her landmarks and pressed over McBurney's point. She received a vociferous positive.

'Can I use your phone to call for an ambulance?' Sally smoothed her hand over the child's head, sorry that she'd had to cause him more pain. 'I'm afraid it looks as if he's got appendicitis, so we need to get him in quickly.'

'Appendicitis?' The poor woman grew almost as pale as her son. 'I didn't know children could get it.' She indicated the telephone and sat down to comfort her frightened little boy.

'They'll be here in a few minutes,' Sally said as she put the receiver down. 'If you like, I could sit with him while you get a few things together for him.' She could see that the sobbing child was upsetting his mother, and the more upset she became, the more he sobbed.

'What sort of things?' She looked flustered.

'Just a wash-kit and a favourite toy for the time being,' Sally suggested as she sat down beside him and slid him carefully onto her knee to comfort him. 'You'll be able to bring him some clean pyjamas when you come to visit after it's all over.'

Another thought struck her just as the young woman went to leave the room. 'Is your husband at work? Perhaps you'd like to phone him, or leave a message so he doesn't worry when he comes home. . .'

'He's away. He works in the North Sea, on one of the oil platforms.' She dithered, as if she couldn't decide whether to collect her son's belongings or contact her husband.

'If you get things ready for the journey first, you can always phone your husband while the ambulancemen load your son—if they arrive before you're ready.'

Once she'd been given a direction, the mother worked fast, bringing the small handful of items back to the sitting-room and using her son's new school bag to pack them into.

As she made her way around the house Sally could hear her checking that everything but the front door was locked before she finally sat down to dial her husband's contact number.

By the time the ambulance arrived she was much calmer. The tears she'd wept while she was telling her husband what was happening were over, and she was trying to distract her son with messages from his father when there was a noise at the front door.

'Hello?' A familiar voice sounded in the hallway and Luke's footsteps approached the sitting-room. 'Somebody told me there was a young man waiting in here who's going to have a special ride with me. Has anybody seen him?'

Sally laughed as the awful tension in the room disappeared like a puff of smoke.

'Who's he?' her young patient whispered, with eyes growing larger by the minute as Luke stepped into the room.

'Are you my passenger?' Luke squatted down so that his head was on the same level, obviously knowing that at six feet tall he was a very impressive height to a small child.

He held out a large hand. 'Hello. I'm Luke,' he smiled.

There was a tiny pause before a small paw was placed trustingly in his palm.

'H'lo. I'm Gary,' the child echoed.

'Shall we let your mum come for the ride with us?' Luke whispered. 'Has she been a good girl?'

There was a little giggle and a nod.

'Well, then, sir. If I can whisk you off on my magic carpet. . .' Luke retrieved the blanket he'd deposited on the floor beside the settee and flicked it out as if he was covering a table with a cloth. 'Climb aboard,' he invited, then wrapped the sides around the little body and Sally at the same time.

'Oops. Too many bodies.' He pulled a comical face and slid his arms into the narrow space between the two of them, his knuckles grazing right across Sally's ribs before he swept Gary up in his arms.

'Are you going to carry my mum, too?' Gary was so intrigued by Luke's nonsense that he'd almost forgotten his fear and his pain.

'I think we'll let your mum and the doctor carry each other out. . .' A sweet, childish giggle floated back towards the two women as Luke carried the boy out towards the front door. 'Come along, ladies, your carriages await,' he called as he left the house.

'I would never have believed it,' Gary's mother marvelled as she picked up belongings and her own handbag. 'One minute he was crying, and the next he's treating the whole thing as an adventure. Are all ambulancemen like that?'

'They're all very good. . .' Sally smiled as she finished her thought in her heart—but Luke Nemo's definitely special. One of a kind.

The rest of Sally's visits were relatively uneventful, and she was starting to look forward to her supper when the mobile phone rang.

'Dr Webster, we've had a call from Mrs Sillitoe. It's about six weeks since her last period, and she's just had her pregnancy confirmed. She's having crampy pains and she's started spotting.'

Sally's heart sank.

Jean Sillitoe had been so pleased to be told she was pregnant. Now she had the classic diagnostic triad for an ectopic pregnancy.

'I'm on my way,' Sally confirmed. 'Send the ambulance to load-and-go. I'll meet them at the hospital with her notes. Can you warn Gynae we're coming? I don't want her to rupture, or we could lose her as well as the baby.'

She did a swift turn in a side-road and started back towards the surgery, superstitiously crossing her fingers that Jean would be all right.

It could only have been a fortnight or so ago that she'd sat in the consulting-room beaming with delight.

'I never thought it would happen to me,' she'd confided shyly. 'I nursed my mother through MS until she died, then Father had a stroke and I couldn't leave him. Colin and I have waited nearly twenty years for this day. . .'

And now it looked as if the dream was all going wrong.

'How is she?' Sally panted when she joined Luke at the door of the emergency department as he pushed the trolley through to meet the reception committee.

'She's been vomiting, her temperature and pulse are raised, she's pale and clammy and there's severe localised pain on the right side.'

'How much is she losing?' Sally quizzed as she raced after them.

'Very little.' He stopped as the patient was transferred to the care of the hospital staff and faced her. 'I've got a feeling about this one, Sally,' he said seriously. 'I don't think this *is* a tubal pregnancy. I think it's another appendicitis.'

'What?' Sally blinked. 'But the spotting. . .?'

'It happens in a percentage of normal pregnancies.'

'Oh, Luke.' She grabbed his hand and held on tight for a moment, her heart lifting with hope. 'I do hope you're right.' And she whirled away to find out what was happening to Mrs Sillitoe, turning back towards him as she reached the door.

'Will I see you later?' She made sure her words sounded casual.

'Decaffeinated?' He raised one eyebrow and his eyes smiled wickedly. 'I'll even let you drive me home.'

CHAPTER NINE

SALLY was nearly floating when they arrived home an hour later.

'She's going to be all right, Luke. You were quite right about her appendix.' She laughed gaily as she danced down the hall and into the kitchen, Amber cavorting noisily around her legs.

'She's not out of the woods yet,' Luke warned. 'She's got a long way to go—not least getting over having her appendix removed.'

'But I was convinced she'd lose the baby anyway, and they'd have to try again.'

Amber was silent now, concentrating on the important business of eating, and Sally straightened up to lean back against the edge of the sink.

'For some stupid reason it hadn't occurred to me that the surgeon would be able to do keyhole surgery in spite of the pregnancy.'

'Ah, progress,' Luke sighed dramatically, and Sally threatened to flick him with the corner of the teatowel.

They took their coffees through to the sitting-room and sat on the settee, as comfortable in each other's company as if it had only been yesterday that they'd last sat there and exchanged news and views, with the soft lighting just enough to make the room feel cosy.

'How is the computerisation coming along?' Luke questioned as he stretched his feet out under the coffee-table and sprawled back into the soft upholstery of the corner.

'I think we're finally getting there.' There was relief in her voice. 'Today I actually had a whole surgery without anything going wrong with it.'

He laughed lazily and she relished the sound, could imagine all too easily that this scene was a part of her future—their future.

She smiled as she remembered his nonsense game with young Gary today. It had been an inspired way to take the fear out of a potentially terrifying situation for such a young child. With a little pang she realised that it was just another admirable side to a many faceted man—evidence that he would be a wonderful father to his own children.

A warmth spread through her at the mental image of Luke playing with his own children—their children—and she imagined herself carrying them, nursing them. . .

'What's the matter?' The long hand lying along the back of the settee stroked her hair, tangling in the uncoiled strands as he combed his fingers through the silky length. 'You had a strange expression on your face. . .'

'Just thinking. . .' She paused, not quite daring to tell him the exact nature of her thoughts. 'About Mrs Sillitoe and her baby, and about young Gary. . .'

'A good day.' He smiled too. 'An all's well that ends well sort of day, with the satisfaction of knowing that you've done the best you can. . .' His voice trailed away, the tone making Sally's sensitive antennae twitch.

'Is that what you want, Luke?' she asked softly. 'The sense of satisfaction at the end of the day? Is that what you became a paramedic for?'

'Perhaps. I don't really know.' He shrugged. 'At the time I just saw it as something I could do to repay the help I'd been given until I could return to my old life—whatever that was. . .'

'Then you're very lucky,' she commented, drawing his eyes to her. 'By nothing more than coincidence, you chose something that you're superb at. Your instincts are amazing.'

She watched the slow red tide spread over his cheekbones as embarrassment and pleasure mixed in his face, and she ached to draw him into her arms—ached to have the right to enfold him in her love and tell him how much she cared.

'How has the decorating been coming along? Have you nearly finished now?'

Sally sent up heartfelt silent thanks as Luke found something else to talk about. If he'd asked her what she was thinking just then. . .

'I haven't had much free time lately, so it hasn't got nearly as far as I'd hoped.' She pulled a face.

'You've finished the ground floor, though, haven't you? It looks really good.'

'*Anything* would look better than the state it was in when I moved in,' she said with feeling.

'*Anything*?' he teased. 'I seem to remember a rather abortive attempt at papering going on in this room the first time I saw it. . . Oi!' He ducked to avoid the scatter cushion she was trying to hit him with.

'That was wonderful in comparison with the original, I'll have you know. An old lady had lived here for years, and when she couldn't cope alone any more it was put on the market. I was the first person to dare to take it on in the state it was in.'

Luke raised a sceptical eyebrow, and Sally was stung into proving her point.

'Come on, then.' She grabbed his hand and tugged, trying fruitlessly to pull him up off the settee. 'You come and see what the upstairs is like. I haven't had a chance to do much up there. You'll see.'

She turned and marched away, her shoulders stiff as she led the way up the uncarpeted stairs.

'There you are.' She pushed open the door of the tiny bathroom and walked in, flicking on the bare lightbulb hanging from the centre of the ceiling. 'It's been scrubbed and bleached, so at least I know it's clean, but do you see what I mean?' She gestured with her hands as she turned to face him. He paused in the doorway and she saw his face fall.

'I suppose it's wonderful, if you like slime-green.' He grimaced at the grim state of the decoration, and walked in to turn around and see the rest of it.

Sally drew in a swift breath as he brushed against her, the space in the cramped room seeming to shrink with his powerful presence.

For the first time since she'd moved in, there was the scent of the last lingering remains of male toiletries in the room—and the presence of the man wearing them.

He was forced to stand so close in the enclosed space that she had to look up at him—up past the broad shoulders to the dark hair just starting to curl over the edge of his collar at the back.

Her fingers tightened into fists as she fought the temptation to reach up and run them through the silky strands, and she stammered into speech.

'Do. . .do you want to see the rest of it? I. . . I've tried to get it in some sort of order, but it's still pretty much in the state I—'

'Lead on,' he invited, cutting through her babble with an amused grin, and inviting her to go past him.

'The guest-room,' she announced defiantly, daring him to laugh at her sudden nervousness.

It wasn't her fault that she was so aware of him when they brushed past each other. It wasn't her fault that she'd had so little real experience of men that she didn't know whether it was possible for her to take the initiative, or even whether she would have the nerve to tell him how she felt about him.

She also had no idea how he would react if she did tell him, and that was the real reason why she hadn't dared.

'Good God.' Luke's horror-filled voice broke into her feverish thoughts as ornate wall-lights illuminated the room. 'Did this lady suffer from some kind of mental illness?'

He looked up at the deep purple ceiling, then around at screaming orange walls. 'You ought to supply sun-glasses before you bring anyone in here.' He blinked and shook his head.

'Apparently she was a very. . .frugal. . .lady, who only bought paint when it was sold cheaply as stock clearance. The same thing went for the tiles in the bathroom.'

'I noticed that each wall was a different design.' She could hear the amazement in his voice as he looked around at the room. 'What about the next one?'

'This one's quite tame by comparison.' Sally pushed open the door and flicked the light on in the little box-room—the one she'd fantasised about turning into a nursery, because it was right beside her own room. . .

'Flamingo-pink.' Luke chuckled. 'Everywhere—ceiling, walls, woodwork. . . Everything is flamingo-pink.'

'Except my boxes.' She pointed out the heap of cardboard containers stacked along the walls. 'They're full of all the things that haven't found a home yet—and some of the things I haven't had time to unpack.'

'They're probably the only things that could survive

living in this room without going mad.' Luke laughed, turning to lead the way to the final door.

'That's. . .' Sally put a hand out to stop him going into the last room, her bedroom, but she was too late.

He had already switched on the apricot shaded light and was walking across the thick silvery sage carpet she'd chosen, towards windows which looked out at the same view as her kitchen.

'This is lovely.' His voice was quiet as he turned to rest his hips against the windowsill and look around at the room, the soft apricot light seeming to deepen the tones of his skin to bronze.

He looked admiringly at the tones of apricot and sage in the curtains and upholstery of her bedroom chairs, and the accents of terracotta in the cushions and curtain-ties which linked the colour scheme to the rest of the house. For the first time she realised that it toned with his colour scheme too, but couldn't remember whether she'd chosen it after she'd visited his house or before.

'It's a beautiful mixture of warmth and calm—just like the woman who chose it.' His brief glance towards her was almost a caress.

Finally, he focused on the bed—her bed—where she'd spent far too many nights dreaming of him.

'And she's a romantic,' he teased in a husky voice as he admired the gleaming brass of the rails at head and foot and the hand-worked patchwork quilt draped over it.

Sally's pulse was racing so fast that her heartbeats seemed to merge into each other, her whole body quivering with tension. The situation was so intimate—having Luke in her bedroom admiring her bed. Too intimate. Especially when he was looking at her with eyes of whisky fire.

'Sally?' The whisper seemed to echo endlessly in the room, drawing her towards him as if she'd been mesmerised by those eyes. 'Ah, Sally. . .' His deep voice grew rough as he reached out to her and folded her in his arms.

She nestled against him willingly, her arms circling his lean waist, and discovered that he was shaking too—a fine tremor that told her that he was as affected by her touch as she was by his.

'Oh, Luke.' She tilted her head back to gaze up into his face, and saw the look of fierce concentration just before he brought his mouth down on hers.

His expression had told her to expect fierce power, but what she found was sweet tenderness as he brushed his lips over hers. The tip of his tongue painted moisture over the fullness of her lower lip, and the silky slide as he deepened the contact between them was perfection.

She moaned softly as her head dropped back, her neck no longer able to hold its weight as her growing arousal dictated her instinctive submission.

Her neck was bared, vulnerable to his plundering mouth as he murmured wordlessly against the sensitive tissues, his body growing more tense as hers grew boneless.

'Beautiful,' he praised as his hand slid inside her flimsy bra to cup her swelling warmth. 'Perfect,' he breathed, and she watched, spellbound, as his mouth replaced his fingers at her nipple, drawing her into his dark warmth as she'd imagined his child doing.

'Luke!' she cried softly, her hand cradling his head against her as he suckled her, the sharp twist deep inside her womb unexpected, startling.

It was like a key unlocking a secret door. That first spear-thrust of arousal sent a river of hot sweet honey surging through her, warming her, making her feel moist and heavy, swollen in intimate places.

As if he knew what she was feeling, Luke's hands were stroking her, caressing her, smoothing her clothes from her body just as she became convinced that she couldn't bear their barrier to his touch.

Shyly she fumbled with the first of his shirt buttons, her eyes avid for the sight of his body now that she had his tacit permission to touch, to admire, to arouse.

Her exploration was tentative at first, as she tried to mimic what he had done to her.

His chest was broad, the muscles flat and firm, the dark whorls of hair drawing her eyes and her fingers towards the dusky nipples half hidden by them.

'God!' Luke jerked as she nipped the tiny bead between her lips, the way he'd done to her.

'Don't. . .don't you like it?' she whispered, stroking soothing fingers over it and feeling him quiver.

'Ah, Sally, I like it too much,' he groaned, and cupped the back of her head to draw her mouth back up to his.

'You're a sorceress,' he whispered against her lips. 'You've taken control of my body until I can hardly think what I'm doing.' And he plundered her mouth, his tongue duelling with hers, sliding in an erotic battle which both could win.

Sally made an awkward first attempt at releasing the waistband of his trousers, her fingers trembling wildly as she anticipated smoothing her hands over the contained power of his thighs and buttocks.

'Help me, Luke,' she moaned. 'I can't. . .'

'Come here, sweetheart.' His voice was husky with arousal as he led her to the side of her bed. He flicked the quilt aside and tenderly laid her down, the sheets cool against her bare skin.

Before she could think about being embarrassed he was sliding away the silky scrap of her last garment, then he stood proudly beside her and slid the last of his own clothes away.

'Oh, Luke.' She held her arms out towards him. 'You're even more beautiful than I remembered.' Her eyes travelled over him, from the distinguished set of his head on his shoulders to the lean power of his torso and the blatant potency of his manhood.

She felt her cheeks colour as she gazed at him in all his glory.

'Blushing, Sally?' he teased gently as he lay down beside her, his weight on the mattress tipping her against the searing heat of his body. 'Ah, God, let me hold you.' And he wrapped her tightly in his arms.

Sally's nervousness disappeared the instant she realised that, in spite of his veneer of control, Luke was still trembling, just as she was, and she held him close to her body.

His face was buried in her hair and she felt him draw her scent in with a deep breath, as though to savour it.

'You always smell so sweet,' he murmured, his breath tickling her ear.

'And you smell so. . .so male.' She tightened her arms around his shoulders, pressing her aching breasts against the taut muscles of his chest.

Slowly, almost as if it was a dream, her hands started to wander over his body, caressing, exploring, arousing.

As if he guessed her inexperience, Luke was allowing her to set the pace, his own hands and lips following her lead until she reached the limits of her experience.

'Please, Luke.' She was quivering as she begged for him to take control. 'Please. . .I want. . .' She tightened her hands around his shoulders and pulled gently, showing him what she wanted when she couldn't find the words.

'Is this what you want?' he murmured as he lifted his body into the cradle of her hips and brought his chest down to tantalise the aroused peaks of her breasts.

'Yes,' she hissed ecstatically as she felt his power between her legs for the first time. 'Oh, yes.' And her hips tilted helplessly towards him, telling him what she needed to make her feel complete.

He arched above her, probing delicately, and she parted herself for him, her trust in him absolute.

'Oh, Luke, I love you,' she breathed fervently, unable to hold the words back any longer.

Instantly he grew still, frozen in position as though turned to stone, before he swore harshly and twisted away from her.

In seconds he was across the room, his rigid back towards her as he thrust himself roughly into his scattered clothes.

'Luke?' Sally whispered, stunned into immobility by the speed of events. 'What's wrong? What did I do?'

The pain of another rejection was making her feel sick.

Already her softly aroused flesh was growing cold, and she shivered convulsively as she drew the quilt over her naked body.

The only sound in the room was Luke's harsh breathing as he finished dressing, the rasp of his zip as he tucked in his shirt-tails obscenely blatant in the seething silence.

'For God's sake.' She struggled to sit up without uncovering a single inch. 'At least tell me why?' There was a touch of hysteria in her voice as it rose uncontrollably. 'It's not as if it's the first time I've been rejected. . .'

Her words disappeared in a sob, and she knew that it wouldn't be long before she lost what little control she had over the tears massing behind her eyes.

'Get out,' she spat, holding herself rigid as pride briefly came to her rescue. No crying. Not again.

'Sally. . .' He took a step towards her, his hands held out appeasingly, his face quite white.

'Stay away from me. Go on. Get out of my house and don't come back.' Her shaky voice was rising towards a scream.

'What are you waiting for? To see if you can make me cry, make me beg? Oh, no! I did that once and it got me nowhere. I learnt that lesson, even if I forgot the first part. Don't trust men. . .' She shuddered to a halt, her throat too tight to continue as she averted her eyes from him.

She'd trusted Luke. She'd believed that he cared for her.

'Sally, don't. . .' Through the haze of her anguish it almost sounded as though Luke was in torment too. 'It isn't like that—'

'Ha!' she interrupted rudely, glaring at him as the pain erupted in an avalanche of words. 'That's what Brian said too. Just before he told me he'd fallen in love with someone else—someone else who was already carrying the baby he'd said he didn't want from me—'

Her control finally broke just as he reached for her. He ignored the frantic flailing of her arms as she tried to push him away, and crushed her against his chest as she sobbed out her grief on his shoulder.

'Shh, Sally. Don't,' he murmured into her hair as he rocked her like a child. 'You'll make yourself ill. . .'

'Why, Luke? Why?' she cried plaintively, with tears streaming down her cheeks. 'Why doesn't anyone want me?'

'They do,' he soothed as he rubbed his cheek over her bent head. '*I* do. But we can't always have what we want. . .'

It took several seconds for his words to penetrate, and several more before she realised the meaning of them, before they slowed the flow of tears.

Slowly she drew away from him until she could see his face. He looked as haunted as she felt, as though the only difference in their grief was the fact that she was crying visibly while he wouldn't allow himself to.

'Then, why?' she demanded in a choked voice. 'Please, Luke. Tell me why.'

'Because I can't,' he said in an arid voice, his shoulders slumping as though they carried a heavy load.

'But. . .' Before Sally could control the impulse, her eyes flicked down towards his belt. She dragged them away immediately, her face growing hot when she realised that he had seen the direction of her gaze.

'Not that way.' His chuckle was strained. 'As far as I know, *that's* in working order. You saw for yourself a few minutes ago.' He grew silent, the teasing smile fading from his face. 'It's more basic than that. A matter of honour. . .'

'I don't understand.' Her whisper was plaintive as she wrapped her arms around herself, suddenly discovering that the quilt had fallen around her waist.

Feeling very naked under his sombre gaze, she pulled it up to cover her breasts. 'If I want you, and you want me. . .' Her eyes were wide and vulnerable as she admitted her feelings aloud.

'But I don't know if I'm free to want you. . .!' The words were torn out of him, his tone anguished. 'I don't know if I was engaged before *this* happened.' He stabbed a finger towards his head, but whether he meant the scar or the loss of memory didn't matter. 'I could be married. Somewhere, I could have a family who don't know where I am or why I've never come home.'

Helpless in the face of his pain, Sally let her arms creep around his shoulders and drew him against her for comfort.

'Surely,' she murmured against his silky dark hair, 'surely, if you were married your wife would have been looking for you. If it was me, I would never stop searching until I knew where you'd gone. I'd leave messages with the Missing Persons helpline, the Salvation Army, everyone. . .'

'For all I know, someone might have done just that,' Luke agreed sombrely. 'But as I don't even know my own name, how can I find out?'

His tormented words lingered in the soft apricot light.

Finally Sally found the courage to ask the questions which were burning a hole in her heart.

'What does that mean for us?' The ache inside her coloured her tone with desperation. 'Does it mean you'll never feel free to fall in. . .to make love. . .?' Her voice failed her at the thought of a future empty of dreams.

In silence, Luke stood up and walked over to the window, gazing out sightlessly into the blackness beyond.

Sally watched, her arms wrapped around herself again to contain the awful ache inside.

'I don't know.' The deep voice emerged into the

silence, muffled slightly by the distance between them. 'I hadn't even considered the possibility that I might meet someone. . .'

He turned to face her, and Sally watched him settle his hips back against the windowsill in exactly the same way as he'd done before everything exploded in her face.

'I haven't been out with a woman since I woke up in hospital,' he admitted baldly. 'I haven't wanted to. Until I met you.'

The surge of pleasure at his admission was short-lived.

'So where does that leave us?' Sally concentrated on tracing the pattern of the intricate piecing of her quilt. It hurt too much to look at Luke and see what she was losing.

'I don't know,' he repeated. 'It depends on you.'

'On me?' That brought her head up. 'I'm not the one who might be married. Oh, I'll admit I had a narrow escape, but—'

'Sally, no. That's not what I meant.' His face twisted in a grimace. 'Or maybe it is. As you said, you're free to find someone to love, to marry and have children. I might never be free—of the uncertainty, if nothing else.'

'So?' She drew in a deep shuddering breath.

'So are you willing to take a step backwards to what we had before—the friendship, the companionship—knowing that it can't go any further?'

Sally shook her head, her initial reaction one of denial, but then she took stock of the consequences if she said no. To see Luke in the distance, even work closely with him, knowing that there was an impenetrable wall between them. . ..

There would be no such thing as a clean break with

the two of them living and working in allied professions in the same town.

'I need time to think.' She ran the fingers of one hand through her hair as exhaustion finally overtook her. 'Too much has happened today. My mind is. . .' She shook her head.

He nodded, his face suddenly seeming much older.

'I'll let myself out of the back door and lock it behind me.' He walked towards the bedroom door, his feet almost silent on the thick carpet, then paused with his hand on the brass handle, his face averted from her. 'I'll understand if you feel that you want me to stop coming round. Do you want me to push the key through the letterbox?'

'No,' she said quickly, her heart clenching painfully at the finality of the suggestion, and she gave a helpless little sigh. 'No, not yet. Give me time to think, Luke. We both need to think about the consequences, whatever we decide to do about it.'

'OK.' He sighed and nodded briefly, the light gleaming on the dark strands of hair that she'd run her fingers through as she'd cradled him against her naked breast. . .

Sally squeezed her eyes tightly shut, but even then she could see Luke. He was imprinted on her mind's eye as clearly as if she'd opened her eyes and looked at him—but when she did open them he was gone, her doorway as empty as if he'd never been there.

She concentrated hard, listening for the creak of the bottom stair and the low murmur as he said goodnight to Amber. There was the tell-tale sound of the back door closing, and the click of the tumblers as he turned the key.

Then silence.

Sally cursed herself for her weakness, but she curled

up in a ball under the quilt and cried herself to sleep.

The morning found her with a stuffy head and pink eyes, but a strangely determined mood.

At some time during the hours she'd tossed and turned, her subconscious had lined up all the facts and drawn the only possible conclusion.

Now all she needed to do was tell Luke her decision.

She wouldn't leave a message for him at work; this was a totally private matter, and she didn't want to have his colleagues speculating about him. He'd had enough of that after his accident.

In the end she decided that if she didn't come in contact with him during the day, she would gather her courage up in both hands and go round to see him tonight.

Sue looked at her speculatively when she arrived at the surgery, and Sally wondered if her camouflage job wasn't as efficient as she'd thought. But she didn't say anything, just handed her a pile of correspondence and test results with her usual cheery good morning.

The day was the familiar mix of good and bad, starting with a six-year-old sent to the special diabetes clinic for confirmation of diagnosis and treatment.

This was balanced by a report on an elderly cleric who'd been plagued by urine retention. Having found his prostate very much enlarged, Sally had referred him to a surgeon for a partial removal, worried that it might be prostatic cancer.

The surgeon's confirmation that it had only been benign prostatic enlargement was a welcome relief, as she'd really liked the gentle man with the dry sense of humour.

'Sally?' Sue's tone over the phone was apologetic.

She knew that Sally was just about ready to leave for the day. 'I've got an extra patient out here. She's visiting relatives and she says she's suddenly developed violent tinnitus.'

'OK, Sue.' Sally deposited her bag on the top of her miraculously clear desk. 'Send her in.' She sat down in the chair again, and waited for the tap on the door.

'I'm so grateful, Doctor.' The poor woman seemed to be at the end of her tether. 'It's like a dreadful buzzing in my ear the whole time. I can't hear anything else properly and it's driving me mad.'

'It's no problem.' Sally smiled and fixed a fresh cone to the end of the otoscope before she switched on the little light. 'If you'd just like to hold your hair away from your ear, I'll take a look. Is the buzzing in both ears?'

Sally made certain she was facing the patient when she spoke, in case she needed the extra prompt of watching her mouth to decipher her words.

'No. Just this one.' She pointed, and Sally bent towards her.

'Ah,' Sally said, in true doctor-fashion when she saw the problem. 'If you'll just wait here a minute, I need to get another piece of equipment.'

She was chuckling as she stuck her head round the door of the treatment room.

'Ah, Denise.' She smiled at the nurse busily wiping down the surfaces at the end of a busy session. 'Where do we keep the fly spray?'

'In the cupboard under the sink.' She pointed. 'Have you got a problem?'

'Not for long.' Sally smiled again as she sprayed a little on a cotton bud and returned to her room.

'Right, Mrs Pollock.' Sally gently introduced the cotton bud. 'The noise will probably get worse for a few minutes, but then it should disappear completely.'

'Oh, that would be wonderful, Doctor. But I've heard that once you get tinnitus badly, it never goes away again.'

'Is it any different at the moment?' Sally resisted the temptation to look.

'Oh, yes. It's got much louder. It almost sounds angry.'

'Good.' Sally smiled. 'Not much longer now, then I'll take another look inside.'

When the bemused woman reported that the noise had mysteriously stopped, Sally removed the cotton bud and had another look with the otoscope.

'Ah, yes,' she murmured, and reached for a fine pair of tweezers. 'This was the cause of all the trouble, Mrs Pollock. A tiny fly had got itself stuck, right up near your eardrum.'

'What a blessed relief,' she sighed, then laughed delightedly. 'You wait till I tell my husband. He said it was a sign of old age, and it meant I was ageing faster than he was.' She stood up and held out her hand. 'Thank you so much for seeing me, Doctor.'

There was a burst of laughter at the reception desk when Mrs Pollock regaled them with the story of her miracle cure for tinnitus, but Sally was too busy grabbing her bag and jacket.

She had promised herself that she would go round to speak to Luke this evening, and she was going home first to have a bath and wash her hair. The last time he'd seen her she'd been crying her eyes out and had looked terrible, like some sort of wild woman. This time she was going to look calm and in control of herself.

CHAPTER TEN

'THE best laid plans. . .' Sally muttered darkly as she bundled her wet hair into a ponytail with an elastic band.

She'd just finished rinsing off the conditioner and had sunk up to her neck in her favourite bubble bath when the phone rang.

For one brief moment she'd contemplated drowning the thing in the bath, then she'd leapt out to concentrate on the voice on the other end while trying to pull a tracksuit on her dripping body at the same time.

She shivered as the chilly evening breeze reminded her that she hadn't had time to put underwear on, and thrust her arms into her jacket before climbing into the vehicle and checking her directions.

Within seconds she was on her way, responding to a call from a concerned neighbour.

'Doctor,' A birdlike woman beckoned her over when she reached her destination. 'This window. Look,' She craned her neck round and pointed with a gnarled finger. 'I can see someone in the hallway, but they don't answer when I ring the bell and the telephone is engaged. I'm very worried, doctor. They're such nice people. . .'

Sally was grateful when her guide was distracted by the arrival of a police car. One of the occupants was immediately grabbed for the full recital, but the other escaped to join Sally.

'She's right about it looking like someone in the

hallway,' Sally pointed out. 'Look, you can see a trouser-leg and a hand.'

'We need to get inside,' he said, and led the way towards the back of the house, reporting on his radio that if there was no easy means of access he'd break a window.

While he was looking Sally peered through a window and found herself looking at the kitchen sink.

'Officer,' she called. 'Quickly. I can see an animal stretched out in the doorway.'

Within seconds he'd broken the window and released the catch and was preparing to climb in.

'Give me a leg-up,' Sally suggested swiftly when she gauged the comparative sizes of the window and his shoulders. 'I'm smaller.'

'Get the back door open as quickly as you can, in case it's gas. Take a deep breath before you go in.'

Sally did as he said, actually holding her breath for the time it took to scramble down from the top of the sink and across to the back door.

'The key was in the lock,' she reported as she swung the door wide and came out for her bag.

'Wait outside while I get the front door open,' he demanded. 'If it's gas, we don't want you going down as well.'

'OK,' Sally nodded. 'But hurry. . .'

The other emergency services must have arrived at the front, because there was a sudden influx of bodies into the house, the fire crew wearing breathing apparatus while they went right through the building opening windows.

As soon as she was given clearance Sally sped inside to the man in the hallway, reaching him at the same time as an ambulance team from the opposite direction.

'Take him straight outside and get him on hundred percent oxygen,' she directed, knowing he was in good hands.

There was a shout behind her, and she looked up to find a fireman coming down the stairs with a young child draped across his arms.

'There's another one up there. Left-hand bedroom,' he shouted, his speech hampered by his breathing equipment. 'I'll take this one out to the ambulance.'

Sally didn't wait to see him go, her feet already flying up the stairs.

The child she found must have been the twin of the one already carried out, and her face was deathly pale. Sally managed to lift her off the bedroom floor and grab her bag again with a speed she hadn't known she possessed. She whirled round and made her way back to the top of the stairs and started down again, her pulse starting to race and her breathing growing laboured.

'Give her here.' Luke's tall frame materialised in front of her and plucked the child out of her arms. 'Get out of here, fast,' he ordered, and turned to take the stairs at a run, leaving Sally to stumble out behind him.

'My legs feel as if they're made of rubber,' she muttered as she sat down for a second on the front wall of the property. 'I'm not as fit as I thought if running upstairs can take it out of me like that.'

'You fool!' Luke's face appeared from nowhere, and he grabbed her by the shoulders and shook her. 'One of the most important rules when dealing with gas leaks is that you never go in without breathing apparatus.'

'But all the windows were open,' she protested.

'And the gas was still leaking.' He pulled her upright and swung her off her feet.

'Hey!' she squeaked, only just retaining her hold on her bag. 'Put me down!'

'Not 'till I'm ready,' he growled, and carried her up the steps of the ambulance. 'Sit down and sit still,' he ordered as he reached across for a mask connected to the fixed oxygen system and held it against her face.

'Didn't anyone ever tell you that dead heroes can't save lives, and injured heroes are a nuisance?' The anger in his face softened as he stroked some straggly strands of hair away from her cheek with a gentle finger.

Suddenly Sally remembered that her hair was tied back in a rough bunch, probably still soaking wet, and she was wearing an old tracksuit without a stitch underneath it.

'I look a mess,' she mumbled, and Luke laughed.

'Now I know you're all right. You can always tell with women, as soon as they start worrying about their looks.'

'Not necessarily, Luke Nemo,' she murmured as she pulled the mask away from her face.

She took a quick look around for eavesdroppers, but they were alone for the moment, the other ambulance having departed with the three victims.

'As far as you're concerned, any woman from nine to ninety would sit up and take notice—and a few either side of those ages.'

She laughed as she saw him colour with embarrassment, and stood up carefully. For some strange reason, she felt she needed to be upright when she broached the next topic.

'Are you going to be off duty tomorrow evening?' she queried. 'Only I'd like to talk to you.'

His eyes bored into hers, as though he wanted to read her mind, but she kept her expression neutral.

She'd wanted to speak to him tonight, but after this incident she'd feel better if they both had some time to calm down.

'I'll come round about half-past seven, shall I?' he said politely, his shoulders going back as though he was preparing himself for a firing-squad.

'Unless I'm out on call, that'll be fine.' Sally smiled equally politely and stepped down out of the ambulance.

By six-thirty the following evening, she'd washed her hair and had a bath without the phone ringing. Now she was dressed in a clean pair of jeans and a favourite Aran jumper, with her hair brushed and shiny.

She was just trying to decide whether to twist her hair up to give herself a little touch of sophistication, or leave it down the way Luke liked it, when the phone *did* ring and her heart sank.

'Car crash,' the voice detailed. 'Single vehicle involved. Single occupant trapped and injured.'

This one was a bit further away than the call-outs she'd had so far. On a comparatively straight road with some deceptively sharp bends half hidden behind banks and hedges.

The police were already at the site of the accident when she arrived, and an officer was able to brief her on what they'd found out so far.

'She's conscious and fairly alert, but in a lot of pain from injuries to her leg.' He glanced down at his notes. 'She seems to have wandered off the road and hit a concrete gatepost. The car then swung round and slid backwards into the ditch.'

Sally signalled her thanks and approached the car. 'Meg Royston? I'm a doctor. Can you tell me where you hurt most?'

In between her examination and the fire crew's dismemberment of the driver's side of the car Meg told Sally about the terrible row she'd had with her husband, which had resulted in her driving away to stay with an old schoolfriend.

'I shouldn't have been driving,' she cried as she waited for the analgesic to take effect. 'I could have killed other people instead of just hurting myself and writing off the car.'

'How did you come to crash?' Sally queried. 'This isn't one of the worst stretches on this road.'

'I was crying, and I couldn't see where I was going,' she sobbed. 'We said such terrible things to each other, and Janey was so upset.'

'Is that your daughter?'

'Yes. I was going to bring her with me, but he said. . .' She sniffed and continued, 'Derek said I could go, but I wasn't to take her away with me. God, I'm glad I didn't.'

She looked around her as the driver's side door was removed so that she could be lifted out without doing any further damage. 'If she'd been in here, she'd probably be dead by now.'

It wasn't long before she was loaded into the ambulance and on her way to hospital.

'Just the clean-up left to do,' one of the ambulance crew commented as Sally carried her bag back to her own vehicle. 'The tow truck will be here soon, to load the wreck up, and within a few days you won't know it ever happened.'

Sally wished him a good night and opened her door.

Amber greeted her with a little whine to signal her need of a short business trip, and Sally stood aside to allow her to jump down.

For a couple of minutes she walked busily backwards

and forwards along the grass verge, until she chose her spot then started back towards Sally and the open door.

Suddenly she stopped in her tracks, her ears pricked as though she'd heard something.

Sally watched her in the glow of the last rescue vehicle's emergency lights as she turned round again and started trotting swiftly towards the wrecked car.

'Amber!' Sally called, surprised by the dog's out of character behaviour, and surprised again when she refused to come back when Sally called.

She'd begun walking towards her, wondering what had got into her, when Amber started barking sharply at the car.

'What's the matter, girl? Don't you like them when they've been carved up?' She caught a faint whiff of smoke, and shivered at the thought of what could have happened here tonight.

Meg Royston had several months of pain ahead of her, with a broken thigh, possible fractured pelvis and scars for life as a reminder. But at least she was alive.

'Amber!' she called more sharply as she saw her disappear down into the ditch. 'Come out of there. If the car shifts, you could get squashed.'

The only reaction from the dog was a renewed burst of barking, this time reinforced with whines, as though she wanted to be let in somewhere.

'What's the matter with the dog, Doc?' someone called from behind the lights. 'What's she found? A rat?'

Suddenly the penny dropped.

'Quick. Come here,' she shouted. 'I think there's someone else in the car.'

'Can't be,' another voice shouted back. 'She said she was alone in the car.'

'I think her daughter's in there,' Sally called as she

slithered down the slope towards the back of the car half buried in the ditch. 'I think she hid without her mother knowing.'

'Bloody hell!' someone swore, and there was the sudden clatter of running feet across tarmac.

'Janey?' Sally called, remembering her name from her mother's tearful tale. 'Can you hear me, Janey? Can you tell me where you are?'

For several seconds everyone was quiet as they listened for a reply but there was nothing.

'Amber,' Sally called. 'Here, girl. Show me where she is. Find her, Amber. Find her.'

With a sharp bark the willing animal leapt into the gaping hole where the driver's door had been, and Sally tracked the waving plume of her tail as she squeezed towards the back of the car and climbed onto the misshapen back seat.

'Where is she, girl? Can you see her?' Sally called, trying to peer through the side windows to see if she was trapped on the floor of the car behind the front seats.

Amber pawed at the upholstery in the back of the car, as if she was trying to get through it, uttering little yips of excitement as though she was close to what she was looking for.

'She's in the boot of the car,' Sally confirmed. 'Can you pull the car out of the ditch to open it up?'

'It'll take a few minutes to hook it up,' someone called back. 'Can you speak to the kiddie and tell her what we're going to do so she won't panic?'

Sally waved her agreement and crouched down beside the car, her feet squelching in several inches of mud and petrol at the bottom of the ditch and that same charred smell drifting over her. Was she never going to look her best when she saw Luke?

'Janey? Can you hear me?'

'Ye-es,' sobbed a tearful voice.

'We're going to get you out of there in a few minutes, sweetheart. Are you hurting anywhere?'

'I've got a bump on my head and I think it's bleeding.' She sniffed loudly. 'My hair's all horrid and sticky.'

'Don't worry about it, sugarplum. I'll have a look at it as soon we get you out. I'm a doctor.'

'O-OK,' she hiccuped. 'Doctor?'

'Yes, Janey?'

'Is my mummy. . .? Is she all right? She's not. . .?'

'She's going to be fine, Janey. She's hurt her leg, and she's on her way to hospital at the moment in an ambulance, but she'll be all right soon.'

Out of the corner of her eye she saw another ambulance pull up, and was amazed that enough time had passed for a second unit to have been dispatched since they'd discovered Janey's presence in the wreck.

There was a heavy tow truck positioned in front of the car, and there were various clanks and rattles going on under the bonnet as the cables were attached ready for winching.

'Doctor?'

'Yes, sweetheart?'

'There's a horrid burning smell in here, isn't there?'

Sally sniffed the air.

Suddenly she realised that, instead of dissipating, the smell that she'd thought had something to do with dismantling the car to get Janey's mother out was actually growing stronger, with the peculiar odour that came from electrical things.

'Oh, my God!' Sally leapt to her feet and scrambled frantically for the open doorway. 'Amber!' she ordered sharply. 'Here, girl. Out here, now!'

She saw the dog's tail go down, but Amber obeyed instantly. 'Sit. Stay.' Sally ordered again, and put her bag down beside her to make sure. 'Guard,' she said firmly, pointing to the bag, and whirled to climb into the wreckage herself.

'Fire!' she called over her shoulder, suddenly realising that she had half an army of specialists within a stone's throw of the car. 'The electrics are on fire.' And she clambered into the back of the car.

'Sally! Get out of there. What the hell do you think you're doing?'

Luke's voice blasted her from close quarters, angrier than she'd ever heard him, but it was wonderful to know he was here.

'Get something to pull the back off this seat, Luke,' she gasped, hampered by lack of space as she tried to wrestle with the slippery upholstery.

'Get *out* of there, woman,' he roared. 'Let someone who's trained for the job take over.'

'There isn't time, Luke. No one else is small enough to get in the back here and the car's sitting in petrol, so stop shouting and help me.'

The car tilted as it took his weight, and suddenly he was there, with a long metal implement of some kind in his hand.

'Here.' His voice was raspy. 'Hook one end around the corner and see if you can lever it away from its moorings.'

Sally did as he said, but it didn't seem as if she quite had the strength to wrench it free.

'Position it again.' Luke's voice was almost in her ear as he stretched across the remaining front seat. 'When you're ready, we can pull together.'

'Ready,' Sally panted, catching sight of a twist of smoke out of the corner of her eye. 'Now.' And there was the sound of something snapping.

'Again,' Luke ordered. 'Move it along and try again.'

'Ready,' she said, and there was another wrench.

'Last time, and make it good,' Luke said, and with their final effort the back of the seat canted forward several inches.

'Janey, love,' Sally coaxed. 'Can you squeeze yourself out this way? It'll be much quicker. . .'

A little hand appeared over the top of the seat, and Sally held it reassuringly for a second.

'Out you come, sugarplum,' she said, glancing fearfully over her shoulder at the steady stream of smoke issuing from the shattered dashboard. 'There's an ambulance waiting to take you to the same hospital as your mummy.'

Sally hooked her hands over the top edge of the seat and strained to pull it towards herself, to give the child enough room to escape.

'Clever girl,' she praised. 'You're coming out of there like toothpaste out of a tube.'

She grasped Janey under her arms and pulled her legs through, then swung round to pass her to Luke.

'Quick. Get her out of here,' Sally ordered as the smoke suddenly blossomed into flames.

'You too, Sally. Don't hang about.'

As he backed out of the ruined doorway Sally caught a glimpse of him, the floodlights bleaching all the colour out of his cheeks so that his eyes looked like black coals in his face, then he was gone.

She wriggled round to follow his route out of the vacant doorway when suddenly there was a burst of sparks, and the whole of the dashboard lit up like a firework display, and she didn't know how to get out.

'Luke. . .!' she choked. 'Help! I'm trapped. . .!'

'Cover your face.' His voice shouted to her over the crackling roar of the fire. The smoke had grown too thick to see through, in spite of the open doorway, and it was getting difficult to breathe, but she ducked her head down inside the collar of her jacket in time to avoid the blast of a powerful fire extinguisher.

'Give me your hand, Sally.' His voice sounded closer now, and she reached out blindly towards it, hanging on tight when he grabbed it and pulled her out of the car like a cork out of a bottle.

It was long after nine-thirty by the time Sally finally drew up in her drive.

Luke had taken Janey off to hospital, and she'd known that he'd have work to do to get his equipment ready for the next shift before he would be free to go home.

'I'm tired,' she said aloud, and saw Amber's ears twitch. As she went to climb out of her seat she caught a glimpse of herself. She grimaced and plucked at her clothing. 'And I stink,' she sighed, and dragged herself up the path.

Tired or not, the kitchen was her first stop, with a special treat for Amber and praise for her sharp ears.

Then—the bath.

She glanced at her watch as she took it off. Just three hours ago she'd finished drying her hair and it had looked and smelled wonderful. Now? She screwed up her nose.

She shampooed the terrible stench of burning out of it over the basin and then wrapped a towel around it and stepped gratefully into the bath.

The bubbles closed over her as she sank under them right up to her neck with a sigh.

'Is there room for another one in there?'

Luke's voice startled her so much that she nearly sank under the water, towel and all.

'Luke! What are you doing here? I thought. . . What's that?'

He'd come right into her ugly bathroom and pushed the door shut behind him, pouring two brimming glasses from a familiar dark green bottle.

'One for you, *mademoiselle*.' He stepped forward to offer her one, and set the bottle and the second glass down on the cork-topped stool beside the bath.

'Is it champagne?' Sally tried to see the label, then forgot all about it as she realised that Luke was steadily taking off his clothes. 'Luke!' she squeaked.

'Yes, it's champagne—but you mustn't be greedy. Wait until I join you before you start drinking it.'

'Join me?' Sally breathed as her heart jolted in her chest. 'Luke? What's going on?'

'A celebration,' he said as he casually kicked the last of his clothes aside.

He picked up his glass and leant forward at the waist to touch it to hers with a soft chime. 'Here's to us,' he whispered, holding her gaze as he lifted the glass to his lips and sipped.

'To us,' Sally echoed, and sipped with him, mesmerised by his eyes. They were different somehow. The expression in them had changed.

'Shove up. You're hogging all the bath.'

Hardly realising what she was doing, she sat forward so that he could climb in behind her, seeming to know what to do even though she'd never shared a bath before.

'Ah, Sally,' Luke murmured as he pulled her back to rest in the shelter of his big warm body. 'I thought I was going to lose you tonight.'

'Is that what the champagne's for?' She tilted her

head back to look at him, but she couldn't read his expression upside-down.

'Partly.' He bent forward to drop a kiss on her nose. 'And partly to celebrate rescuing little Janey, but mostly to thank you for being so patient with me.'

'Why?' Sally tried to turn so that she could see his face, but the bath was too small. 'We haven't even had our talk yet.'

'In a way we don't need to have it, because the situation has changed since we spoke the other day. I've changed, and all because you said you loved me.'

'But. . . The other day you said that didn't make any difference. . .'

'I was wrong,' he said plainly. 'I hadn't realised just how much difference it made until I found myself making enquiries about how to dissolve a marriage if you don't know whether you're married or even who you are.'

'Oh, Luke.' Sally twisted awkwardly to look at him, knowing her eyes were full of tears, but this time tears of happiness. 'It might take years to sort out the tangle, but you're worth waiting for.'

She tipped her head back on his shoulder and kissed the angle of his jaw. 'That's the decision I was going to tell you I'd made.'

'Oh, Sally.' He tightened his arms around her and tried to kiss her.

'Oops!' Sally squealed as he forgot the glass in his hand and spilt his champagne over her shoulder. 'That's cold!'

'Dammit! This isn't nearly as romantic as it's made out to be,' Luke grumbled as he put his empty glass down on the stool and retrieved hers. 'Have you nearly finished your bath?' he demanded, scooping warm water over her shoulder to wash any stickiness away.

'Actually, I'd only just climbed in when you arrived,' Sally murmured as his hands continued to pour water over her, gradually washing away the covering of bubbles which had hidden her.

The movement of his hands gradually slowed as she was revealed to him, and her pulse began to beat loudly in her ears.

'Luke?' There was a tremor to her voice.

'Shh, Sally, it's all right. Everything's going to be all right.' He dropped a kiss on one smooth shoulder and tilted her forward.

'Hang on to the towel on your head, I'm getting out.' And he braced his hands on the sides of the bath and untangled their legs before stepping out to grab a towel and wrap it round his waist.

'Out you come.' He unfolded a second towel and held it out to her.

'Um, Luke, I'd rather. . .'

'Come on, woman,' he coaxed briskly. 'You can't hang around in there, turning into a prune. We've got things to talk about. Decisions to make.'

Sally bit her lip and reluctantly stood up, the water and bubbles running down her in glittering cascades.

'Oh, Sally, love.' His eyes darkened as they travelled over her. 'You're so beautiful.' And he stepped forward to wrap the towel around her and lift her into his arms.

'Luke?' she murmured uncertainly as he carried her through to her bedroom and set her on her feet on the rug beside her bed. 'If we're going to talk, wouldn't it be better if—'

The rest of the sentence was consigned to oblivion as his mouth met hers tentatively, tenderly, his lips nibbling and teasing hers until she parted them for him.

Gradually tender exploration became passion, and

Sally gave herself totally into his keeping, trusting him as she'd trusted no one before.

'Sally!' Luke stiffened in shock as their bodies at last became one, and he discovered her final secret.

'I'm sorry,' she whispered. 'I didn't know how to tell you that I've never. . .that Brian didn't even want. . .'

'Sorry? What on earth for? You've made me feel like a. . .like a king.' He kissed her deeply, until the brief pang was forgotten in renewed arousal.

Gradually the fires grew hotter as she followed his lead, touching as he touched, moving as he moved, until they reached the white-hot core together and shattered into infinity.

Sally lay silently, wrapped in Luke's arms. His long lean body warmed her back as she carefully went over the events of the day.

There was a missing piece to the puzzle, something significant that she needed to slot into place so that she could see the whole picture.

Finally, as Luke stirred behind her, she realised what it was and she turned to face him.

'You've remembered, haven't you?' she said softly, her words a statement rather than a question, then held her breath as she waited for his reply.

'Yes.' His smile was different, wider and easier, as if it was something he did often. 'How did you know?'

'You told me.' She gave a little chuckle as he shook his head. 'Not last night, but the night we *didn't* make love,' she said mysteriously.

'But I hadn't got it back then, so how could I have told you?'

'You said your honour wouldn't allow you to make love unless you knew for sure that you weren't committed to someone else,' she explained simply.

'Not only beautiful and sexy, but clever too,' he teased, then grew serious. 'It was seeing you trapped in that burning car that brought it all back,' he murmured, his voice rough with memories.

'You don't have to talk about it if it's too painful, Luke.' She wrapped her arms around him, one hand coming to rest on his scarred shoulder.

'I need to tell you,' he said. 'It's part of my past, and I want you to know.'

'Can I ask a question first?' Sally's curiosity was getting the better of her. 'What was your profession before the accident?'

Luke paused for a moment, then gave her a wicked grin. 'I think, if you don't mind, I'll keep that piece of news till last. I'd like to preserve an air of mystery for a little bit longer.'

'OK.' She pulled a disappointed face. 'It's your secret.'

'It's the only nice secret I've got to tell you,' he said sadly. 'The rest of it. . .'

'Where do you want to begin?' Sally offered, settling quietly in the circle of his arms with her head over the reassuring beat of his heart.

'I was engaged,' he started, and Sally felt a brief stab of sick jealousy. 'We worked together and seemed to have a lot in common. Sandi was American—well, half-American, half-English. Her parents were divorced, and she spent her time being shuffled from one to the other.' He shrugged his shoulders.

'Some people come out of that sort of situation determined and self-reliant. Sandi was weak and clinging, always wanting attention. Unfortunately, I didn't realise it until too late.'

'Where were you working when you met?'

'London. Then I decided I wanted to change my

job, and I had an interview lined up. The one job I *really* wanted. The day before the interview Sandi said she was homesick, and wanted us to go to America to work. She'd lined up some interviews for both of us, and booked tickets without saying a word until almost the last minute.'

He looked down at Sally with hurt in his eyes. 'She'd even phoned to cancel my dream interview. Told them I'd had a better offer!'

'What did you do?' Sally whispered.

'It was too late to do anything about the job I wanted; I told her she could go to America with my blessing, but I wasn't going with her.' He glanced down at her with a grimace. 'We were in a restaurant full of people at the time, but she flung the ring at me and stormed off.'

'But. . .'

'It was one of her favourite tactics, to try to embarrass people into doing what she wanted, but it was the first time she had tried it on me.' He shrugged. 'She came back a few minutes later, demanding that I should take her to collect her bags and then to the airport. She'd phoned her mother, who would be waiting to welcome her with open arms. There was no reason for her mother to suppose that I was with Sandi, given that the engagement was over. And no one else would have been looking for me.'

Sally could feel the tension growing in him, saw the tremor in his hand as he brought it up to rub it over his face.

'I was driving her to catch her plane when it happened. She'd been pouting and crying and generally trying to get me to change my mind. Finally she resorted to screaming at me, and she grabbed the steering wheel. . .' He shuddered and drew in a deep breath. 'We were crossing a busy junction at the time, and there were cars and pedestrians all over the place.'

'Oh, Luke,' she breathed, feeling sick at the thought of all the pain he'd had to forget.

'The car was badly damaged, and burst into flames. I tried to drag her out of the driver's side but she was fighting me, trying to reach her handbag with the tickets and money in it. The last thing I remember is a terrible noise and agonising pain.'

'Little wonder your mind refused to remember it,' Sally murmured, smoothing a comforting hand over the dark silk of his hair.

'But then, if our lives don't take a few twists and turns, we miss out on the beautiful scenery.' He ran the tip of his finger down her profile, from the tangled glory of her hair over her nose and lips to her chin. 'If my life hadn't gone the way it did, I might never have met you.'

He turned onto his side, supporting his weight on one elbow, and cupped her cheek in his palm.

'Will you marry me?' he asked quietly, looking deeply into her eyes. 'I love you so much.' And he lowered his head to press a soft kiss to her lips.

'Oh, Luke, I love you, too.' She ran her fingers through his hair and pulled his head down to deepen the kiss.

'Was that a yes?' He smiled as their lips parted.

'I can't.' She shook her head. 'I don't know who I'll be marrying.'

'Does my name matter to you?' He sounded surprised. 'I can probably choose either, in view of the circumstances. You tell me which you prefer—Luke or Lucas?'

'Lucas?'

'My surname. It must have surfaced from the depths

of the amnesia. I was Adam Lucas. Does it make a difference—?'

'No,' Sally interrupted. 'It's not your name, it's your job I want to know about.'

'And if you don't like what I do, will you refuse to marry me?'

'Not a chance,' she vowed. 'Paramedic or plant propagator—Luke Nemo or Adam Lucas. It doesn't matter. It's you, the person, that I love.'

'What about paediatrician?' he said softly. 'It starts with a "p" too.'

She felt the smile spread over her face.

'Oh, Luke, I'm so pleased for you, my love. I can't imagine anything that you'd be better at.'

'I hope you're right.' He pulled a face. 'It's going to take some time to sort out all my pieces of paper. . .'

'That doesn't matter.' She hugged him tightly. 'Nothing matters now except that you've got your memory back and you can forget all the pain and uncertainty.'

'And I found you,' he murmured as he tilted her chin up. 'Now we can start building a lifetime of memories.' And his lips slowly settled over hers.

How would you like to win a year's supply of simply irresistible romances? Well, you can and they're free! Simply solve the puzzle below and send your completed entry to us by 31st October 1996. The first five correct entries picked after the closing date will each win a years supply of Temptation novels (four books every month—worth over £100).

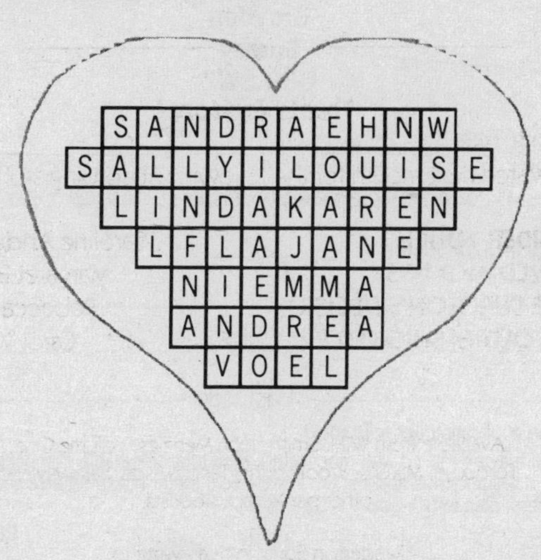

Please turn over for details of how to enter ☞

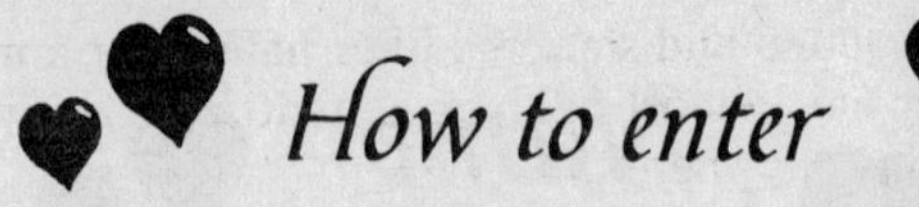

How to enter

To solve our puzzle...first circle eight well known girls names hidden in the grid. Then unscramble the remaining letters to reveal the title of a well-known song (five words).

When you have written the song title in the space provided below, don't forget to fill in your name and address, pop this page into an envelope (you don't need a stamp) and post it today! Hurry—competition ends 31st October 1996.

Mills & Boon Song Puzzle
FREEPOST
Croydon
Surrey
CR9 3WZ

Song Title: ______________________________

Are you a Reader Service Subscriber? Yes ❑ No ❑

Ms/Mrs/Miss/Mr ______________________________

Address ______________________________

____

______________ Postcode ______________

One application per household.

You may be mailed with other offers from other reputable companies as a result of this application. If you would prefer not to receive such offers, please tick box. ❑

C396
D